rania

for Gerrie
this story of early days
which seems now to rouse
much enthusiasm —

in appreciation of her
beautiful willingness to
serve as well as to create

Rudhyar

June 74

RANIA

AN EPIC NARRATIVE

Dane Rudhyar

UNITY PRESS - SAN FRANCISCO

1973

Published Spring 1973 by Unity Press
PO Box 26350
San Francisco, California 94126
ISBN 0-913300-11-X
Manufactured in the United States of America

First Printing

Cover design by Mike Cotten
Back cover photograph by Edward Weston
courtesy of Dane Rudhyar

To Aryel Darma

in memoriam

D.R.

PREFACE

I sub-titled this book "an epic narrative" for it does not belong, in style and in the approach to the characters it portrays, to what is usually called a novel. The term, novel, has been applied, it is true, to a variety of literary productions, and now avant-garde writers are presenting us with "anti-novels"; but RANIA does not belong either to this "new wave." It was written long ago, but at a time of thought-fermentation when some American authors, perhaps stimulated by the German "Expressionism" of the twenties, felt urged to venture into new fields.

The men who won fame in the thirties were content, however, to write characteristically in the novel form, mostly in terms of a realistic approach seeking ever more lurid or dark layers of our chaotic modern society as fields for their psychological and social analysis. I never was attracted by this approach, for I do not believe that it is the creative artist's main function to simply picture in a realistic and detailed manner what he observes around him. I believe that we are living through an age which has much in it that belongs to the "Primitive," a period which represents the closing of a historical cycle. I have often spoken of it as a "seed period." In the seed the essential characteristics of the plant are contained, but in a condensed, hard, stolid manner, haunted, as it were, by futurity. The life of the seed falling on the autumnal soil is a "heroic" life, and ends in the supreme ritual of germination—the gift of self so that future vegetation might be born.

This twentieth century is in various ways a heroic period; not only because of the wars being waged and the crucial social and racial conflicts on the national as well as the international stage, but because the modern individual is confronted in his life—whether he likes it or not—with decisions of a truly epic character. It is true that crucial decisions have had to be made by men and women in any period of history, but in most periods the human being acted within well-defined areas of belief and behavior, and in terms of unquestioned basic loyalties. Not so today. *Everything* must be questioned. There is no really safe solution, at least spiritually and psychologically—even for the youth born to wealth. After having conquered and at times enslaved most of the rest of mankind, Western people are now being faced with the "karma" of their actions, and often their crimes. Western minds are being torn away from all moorings by a spiritual as well as social crisis, the potential fury of which may destroy our society.

I wrote RANIA during the winter of 1930 in Chicago, just after leaving California where I had passed most of ten years in Hollywood and occasionally in Carmel-by-the-sea where I was giving lectures and had devoted friends. RANIA is the story of a strong and unusual woman's life filled with extremes of light and darkness, of beauty and tragedy. I conceived this work as a kind of symphonic narrative in three movements. I emphasized the poetic-musical form by writing at first short stanza-like paragraphs, then, as the action became less tense and precipitated, increasing the length of these stanzas. In the second part of the symphonic-narrative the action slows down, and the stanza-form is no longer needed. It reappears in the third part which ends with a recall of the initial heroic theme of the sacrifice of the seed. In RANIA the action is condensed, often stark, moving from high-point to high-point—today one would probably speak of "peak experiences." The characters are projected on the background of social or natural landscapes which are broadly drawn and essentialized.

Though a number of friends and writers—like Will Levington Comfort—were enthusiastic after reading the manuscript, the publishers who read it felt that this work was too much ahead of its time to reach the broad public which alone interested them. I decided to wait for a more opportune period.

Last year several young friends of mine who read the manuscript insisted it should be published and one of them, Jim Shere, read it in 16 installments over the KPFA Pacifica radio in Berkeley. The response of many who heard the broadcast was extremely warm. Unity Press then offered to publish it and it is felt that the time has come for RANIA to reach the public heart.

FALL 1972

sequence

passionate spring

CHAPTER I

The snow beats against them.

Huge white sheets torn from the skies lash galloping creatures sent through the storm by the haste-call of death. On the other side of the pass, the ghost-fury had not yet reached its full when they heard that fever had clawed him, savage fire amidst the icy wastes. Mother, daughter, they had left. Strong stock, Russian, Magyar, Gypsy . . . mixed strains and fervor of races that plough life to tear from it a harvest of triumphant pain and ecstasy.

The white gale slashes them.

The wolves' barking overtones the winds.

The snow made hunger, black snow moving with instinct, ferocious clang of winter's man-hatred. The horses know; they rebel against the master-hands. They drill madly into raging sails which flap against the white sea of the earth. Wolves, wolves . . . they howl. One jumps, cut back by the lash.

The wolves' hunger overtones the storm.

Big trees have been reached, with easy branches.

The sledge tumbles over roots scarring the snow. The mother, strong and fierce, slashes back the beasts that growl, pushes up the girl climbing the branches. "Hold fast! Peasants will save you after dawn. The farm is near." Bravely she beats, beats the horde that craves her flesh. "Hold fast!" she cries. "Have no fear. Courage, my love! I am strong yet."

Big trees stand like crosses over a grave.

She had been named Rania.

She stood with courage. She was of a strong stock. Her body seemed frozen, her mind deafened by the howlings of the beasts hardly fed by sacrificial flesh. But with power she clung to the ice. She clung to her soul trapped in this fierce planet. She called aloud: "I am not afraid. I am strong yet. I am strong!" And dawn saved her, with kind hands and warm bed from the farm.

She had been named Rania.

Her father recovered.

He was a strange passionate man, with Gypsy blood drawn from old India-lands. Something in him remembered the mounts where saints live who bless mankind with power compassionate and wisdom all-embracing. Something could not forget the lust of torrid plains sickened by fever, reeling with dances of sex, swirling around the brains. And these two clashed and struggled within his violent frame; great knowledge, great fervor, and the strong will of body craving its own against the god.

passionate spring

Her father took her far and away.

Over lands and seas they journeyed.

They reached the New World, where men who are young torture with machines their unborn souls, with greed for power, with rush everlasting. They scoured cities, factories, slums and palaces gilded with blood-dripping money. His many-tongued blood rejoiced in the Babels where all races lust, craving to be reborn as the little children of an earth prolific and strong, where destiny can be met and loved into great deeds and fortunes.

Over states and mountains they tore.

He was a restless soul.

He loved his daughter with a strange passion: that she was beautiful, that she was strong, that she could laugh and dance, yet plundered books for knowledge and gods for divinity. He loved her with a perverse love. He made her face his own debauches. He wanted to feel with her eyes and nerves his own passion. She was stirred, frantic. But she scorned, laughed; and her soul closed her stubborn jaws tight with defiance.

He was a tragic, powerless soul.

One day she saw him beat a young girl.

The girl was beautiful and frail. She had been stranded in some monstrous city and sold herself for bread and the few smiles of things that girls must own. Rania was in her own room; he called her, forced her to witness his shame. He was helpless that day for men had bruised his deepest longings. He must have revenge on life, brutalize bodies to pay for his shattered soul. The girl begged, cried. She tore her hands; she fled to Rania. "Oh! help me!" Daughter faced father in ghastly silence. Dumb confrontation of fates that stood apart, yet rooted in the same earth.

That day she closed the door and left him.

—∞◇∞—

Rania wandered for many days.

She had reached her sixteenth birth. Men stared at her as she passed by for the fervent yet icy splendor of her eyes, the strong, defying pace of her walk that knew direction. She had taken with her but few dollars to start the search. She waited in tearooms; she knew the looks of men stammering over breakfast orders while unable to tear their eyes off her breast. She was assaulted with harrying smiles flushing with covetousness. She danced through music halls amid haggard bodies, and laughed off moist hands already clenching their prey.

Rania wandered, silent, unscathed.

Days and nights she worked, facing life.

Yet her body collapsed under the strain, as she was dancing in a small town. The hospital took her with its white-sheeted peace. For days she was burnt by the violence of the pent up fire within her flesh which had not given up, which had not opened to the craving of men. Then she recovered and was sent to the druggist of the town who needed help, while an official search was made for her father.

And Rania began her new work.

passionate spring

It was at first kind and pleasant work.

She had to wait upon customers hurrying through indigestible lunches, often piercing her clothes with greedy eyes, yet distant and fearful, for the town was small and tongues easy to start. The druggist had a wife, cautious though considerate. She had a strange look, as if ever watching for some ghost to appear from behind things being moved. Her world seemed a shaky world, unsafe; and some troubled longing twisted her upper lip into pain, while her eyes belied suffering with a strange smile.

It was for weeks kind and pleasant work.

A peace-wrapped languor pervaded Rania.

Hospital days had been a long gaze into emptiness, a long waiting, soul-pregnancy in love with the unborn. They had been winter days muffled by snow, gorgeous ermine cloak sheathing the naked blade of sorrow. She had relaxed into expectancy, husband-weary mother loving inward life-to-be. Spring had liquefied the silence into dancing waters. The ermine cloak had shed its fur. Vernal breezes tore through the bethinned fabric and the earth-body stirred into buds like the fields.

The discontent of spring rose in Rania's soul.

Surge of greens, surge of dreams.

He was still a boy. He helped the druggist with his preparations working at night toward college. He was frail and strange-eyed like a deer surprised amid mountain meadows. He looked at life with the same delicacy with which he divided powders into small equal heaps. There was a mystery Rania had not fathomed; but she loved him for his insecureness, for his mother-need.

Surge of greens, surge of dreams.

One night she stumbled over the mystery.

As she stood in the street, breathing the warm spring breeze, she saw the druggist rapidly walking toward the boy's room a few blocks away. He often helped the youngster with his lessons when he had kept him longer than usual at the store. A strange premonition twisted Rania's heart into curious pain. She followed at a distance, waited. The room's curtains were not tight. She could see shadows coming close in the dimmed light.

Her mother-love fathomed the mystery.

Tenderly the little stalk had spun its life sunward.

Now it was crushed once more, with the bitterness of disgust. She understood the writhing lines of pain in the wife; but in herself, it was her heart that bent in awesome loneliness. She wanted to go, but was watched rather strictly. She drew within herself with vehement unearthiness. She hated the earth. She clung to her dreams, wild dreams she had to throw off to bear the contempt and irony of things.

Cypresslike, tense-nerved, she judged life.

Because she was strong she asked for judgment.

It would have been easy to accept and twist the mouth in restrained suffering. But Rania was of a stock of rebels and defiers. She wanted to face life. She did not deny. Her father beating girls, the druggist and his clerk, men, men, men with frenzied hands choking with the longing to pierce and to crush, as if beyond there were God. . . . And if there were God beyond? Was she the weakling? Were they the victorious? Tensely, desperately, she flung questions at the silence of life.

Because she was strong she asked for judgment.

Something answered from within.

It was very faint at first, like translucid steam in a cold room. It shaped itself into moving forms, square, oblong, round . . . somewhere beyond her closed eyes; or was it within the hollow globe? She saw dreams, dreams which she knew were real. She could not grasp the meanings nor the source. But she knew another world had opened and it was a glorious, blazing, yet icy world. She was not frightened, only she could not see the whence nor the whither. Forms and colors were going on; beyond and through. All things, all faces became streaked with strange gyrations.

Was it the answer from within?

She had no one to tell whom she could trust.

She thought at times she was going mad. She thought she was not of the same race of men as others. But she had not the vain pride of men who fool their souls into belief of lone godhood. She passed through days of dreary scorn, as if all her body were spitting upon all men encountered. And it made her so beautiful and wild that men dared not look at her. In the town many words converged toward her. Her father had not yet been found. She was watched. Around her she felt wonder, awe, suspicion.

And no one to tell she could trust.

Yet she loved him.

However much she despised, her youth loved and longed. Two strong streams bounced upon the rocks of pain of her everyday: the mysterious flow of forms and dreams which were like messages unread, letters unopened lying upon the door step, a flow ever more steady and rich threatening to absorb the whole of her in some supernal ecstasy: then the anguish of body, of the want to be loved and to mother, the want to take hands and head into one's own, to forget dreams in the throb of glorious oblivion.

Like a mother, she loved him.

Then she heard her father was coming.

He had been found in a northern city where he had married wealth. First he had refused to bother about her, but decided to send her until of age to a convent in the west. The news struck her, as the druggist's wife confided it. The first thought was: escape. The second, a terrific anger that shattered her bearings and left her powerless and dulled. Then she thought of him, the poor beloved, and his thwarted life against the grain of love.

Soon, soon her father was coming.

If she must go, then victorious.

Life was beating her. She would force life, bow it to her will. Rania, the strong, could not leave, defeated. Face to face she would make destiny, if destiny refused to make life for her. The next day she would be gone. She asked the boy to take her for a last stroll near the river she loved, an upturned sky frowning star-ripples under the strain of the winds.

If she must go, then victorious.

passionate spring

It was late summer.

The trees wept golden seeds into the ceaseless flow of the waters oblivious of their love. The boy was silent, nearly trembling from some fearful ghost, inescapable. In the darkness she took him by both arms; she gazed at him with the passion of wilful love. She cried to him: "Look at me! Look at me! Am I not beautiful? Take me. I shall release you from your curse. I shall drop upon you my strong purity. Grow into me, my boy! Laugh off into me your fear and your ghosts. Ah! take me. . ."

It was late summer.

There were no clouds, nothing hidden.

It was a great fierce gesture of will and strength. She tore him from his shell; she dug into his heart for life to spout and free him who had been slave and bound. She stirred in him the muscular strength that makes the first birth of man toward the second birth of supernal power. As they arose, he was glowing like wild fire with the passion of her in his breast, with the taste of her in his skin. As they arose, he would sing, he would cry, he would dance. She looked at him. She was proud in her fierce motherhood of him as a man.

There were stars, clear, strong, nothing hidden.

The following day she left.

Her father was cold and distant. He had climbed up in the great game of respectability. He was not eager to have his past mar his never-too-safe present. She greeted him with amused scorn. Now, she did not care. She wore red blood over her pale cheeks. Life within pulsed high and rich. She bid the boy good-bye with a triumphant glance. Even the druggist she laughed at, with merry wishes. For her blood knew that in her had come the mystery.

Victorious and fulfilled, she left.

First days in the convent.

Rania entered the gates with laughing defiance. She knew herself powerful and would take it as a test of strength between the life in her and the fallacious benevolence of the grey shells parading silently through endless corridors. She felt the whole atmosphere so ludicrous that it stirred her sense of humor. She faced the frowning nuns with challenging eyes that said: "Here I am. You fools, what will you do with me?" Condescendingly she performed routine work with perfection. The nuns glanced at her, wonderingly, as leisurely travelers at powerful dark bodies hoisting cotton bales in Asiatic harbors.

First days in the convent.

She took refuge in her mystery.

While her body and brains were retailing muscle and nerve tension in ordinary gestures, her soul was sweeping through aeons in great flights of wonderment. In her first sense of motherhood she seemed to have pierced through many crusts, scraping off the dirt of self from the skin of eternity. The great stream of forms and colors which she had beheld in her dreams had taken some inchoate yet deep-thundering meaning in her very fecundation. They were more real, yet less important. They shone now with reflected light like huge moons of some inner skies haloing her heart; but Light itself, the Power, she could sense at the center— streaming, bold, thrilling Light yearning to become form and gesture.

passionate spring

She took refuge in her mystery.

She flung it at her schoolmates.

She faced them, a perpetual mockery aimed at their childish purity, darting poisonous spears at their innocence. She rode through bewildered minds, a fierce Amazon amidst a female herd, slashing prudery and prejudice with sarcasm. A few grew hateful; most worshiped. The irony of her position delighted her, upstrained her. Her acts being reproachless, none could blame her. But her looks and gestures shrieked out her insolent joy.

She flung it at her schoolmates.

And a letter came that shattered all,

The druggist's wife who loved her was writing how the boy-clerk had poisoned himself two days before. No one knew exactly why, save that since Rania had left he had become dreadfully nervous, had made dangerous mistakes in filling prescriptions, had had several angry word-battles with the druggist who was ready to throw him out. His body was resting now at peace under golden oak leaves near the river on which stars were still dancing under the winds.

—∞◇∞—

Then Rania flew into a great passion.

She tore the sheets of her bed.

She beat her womb savagely with terrific laughter.

She jumped from her first story window.

11

Half-numbed by the fall she ran across sloping fields.

Above, rigid mountains heaved frozen sighs

as of some old unbearable pain.

Trees flung themselves many-handed to the sky,

dried up sarcasms of earth-pangs.

She ran to the stables, unleashed a horse

and beat him like mad until the beast,

with foaming mouth, raged with elemental passion.

They tore through ravines and stony fields.

The winter sun stared with hellish fire.

Rania's face reddened with its menace.

Jaws strained, eyes devouring the light,

she was singing, singing, singing.

A wild steppe song of old remembrance

had flared through her brains and body.

She cried it to the darkening skies.

She shouted it to winds gashing through canyons.

passionate spring

Until she and the beast,

spent flames of anger,

collapsed.

All night she lay in the ravine. Her body was bruised and panting, wounded by aborted life. Her body was bleeding like a broken jar; her mind reeling, lashed by words darting through feverish cells: "I have killed him! I have killed him!" Until the sun rose again from the dead, golden and young with triumphant light which caressed her face, which warmed her broken body, which was kind and strong. Rania awoke from the raving stupor and looked at herself, and looked at that other tragic death of the unborn. She smiled, "Poor little one! No chance, this time!"

With great power of will she rose, whistled for the horse which was grazing nearby, unconcerned. She dragged herself upon the beast. She lay panting on his back and rode until men in a car saw her, stopped her and kindly brought her back to the convent.

She lay for weeks with fever.

The nuns were kind and strange, like beings of some other world not yet born, not yet breathing life. They moved gently, noiselessly with feet which had never stamped the pulsating earth. They were still wrapped in grey placenta, floating in the waters of childish belief and obedience. For her who looked with eyes that had known the bleeding of many deaths, they were like phantoms, unreal images of a dreamy limbo. The real, she heard and saw from within her closed burning body. Forms and faces, lights, words rose up, passed through, with meanings of power she felt like electric breaths, yet grasped not.

She lay for weeks with fever.

Strange, dark faces came to her.

With strong clear eyes they beckoned and pointed to great mountains with everlasting snow. They uttered familiar words, words that clanged with fierce majesty. A hidden self that she had never known arose in recognition; a self young and clear, with calm certitude even though its steps seemed so insecure. It moved in the world of forms that glowed from within—curious, geometrical shapes, bars of all colors, spheres, pyramids—swaying with tidal rhythm, yet propelled from within as if they were lives with great hearts beating at their centers.

Strange, dark faces spoke to her.

Slowly the fever left.

She found herself curiously calm and poised. Her eyes, turned inward, smiled with kindness, with amused gentleness at the outward. She was tender to all the grey unborn that paced silently through the halls. She was kind because they knew not, because one must be kind to the future—kind to sleepwalkers also, for fear one might awake them too suddenly and souls might forget the path to the body.

Slowly the fever left.

Something had been born in her.

She knew it from within. She knew it too from the mirror, telling her strange secrets of deepened lines and steadied eyes, of a mouth clear and firm that had been childish and stubborn, but now *lived*.

14

passionate spring

Mysterious life of human mouths! They open to food. They open to breath, and to love. Each time, some of the things that touch the quivering flesh write their names, not to be forgotten. One name after another, one dream, one passion after another. Long years of adolescence ridden through at mad pace, gallopings of proud soul, of heart of ancient stock untamed by the shams of this age. She had killed the still unborn, father and son; and yet. . .

Something had been born that was true.

The Mother Superior spoke to her.

She felt that after all that happened it was better for Rania to leave the convent and go to her father. She had written him and he was coming the next day. Rania answered politely with thanks for the care they had given her. Then, she hesitated as she opened the door. Should she tell words of life to the gentle, indrawn and dulled eyes of a woman who sent her away because she had dared to live and face tragedy? But she smiled, shook her head and then left the sleepwalker to the phantasms of her unformed world.

The Mother Superior stared at her, helplessly.

She met her father at the station.

He seemed older and weighted with unexpressed soul and distrust of life. She faced him in silence. He was almost afraid to look at her strong self which had found power in dying. He asked her at last what she wanted to do. Her stepmother was unkind and spoiled. He did not know whether he could stand it much longer. Money is a poor game to trifle with. He longed for the earth of wild humans raging through steppes and hills. He was yearning for the old earth of his forefathers where men are stolid and bronzed by secrets impenetrable.

She glanced at her father with pity.

But she could not follow.

She too had dreamt of Eastern faces. She knew they would call for her when time had ripened and destiny would speak. But she knew she had to master this, ere that could be reached—this soil of unborn, the mad rush of whitened faces with black sinful souls piercing through the pale joke of civilization. She had killed two unformed lives; she must pay for them with some great heroic birth of a new humanity. She knew life. She knew pain. She knew destiny. She had died within the white lips of beds that led to the greedy mouth of the beyond. But she had come back from below, and she had to prove herself master and mother.

She could not follow him.

He must let her go alone.

The roads were vast and open. She was not afraid. With her own soul she would stamp the earth and she would stamp life. She was not afraid. Somewhere there must be the true father, ready to concentrate his will into her own fruitful soul. If the path had to be through a hundred false fatherhoods and the lies of a thousand lovers, still she would go and falter not. For she was of age now, and not afraid.

He had to let her go alone.

And alone she took the burden of the roads.

He had given her enough to assure her life for a few months to come. He had pressed her into his arms, bowing before the will of the strong stock and the strong soul. He too would go. He was too old to search for true love. He had damned too many with his own lusts and his own cowardice. He had not dared be true to his god. But now he would go, go back whence light came and his own dawn also. He would go back and retrace the rungs of life's hell, and search for peace where glaciers bestow silence and bronzed faces tell no secrets, for they know.

And both took upon them the burden of the roads.

—∞◇∞—

RANIA

CHAPTER II

She went down the coast virescent with spring.

The rust of numberless poppies be-topazed the hills swarming with squirrels. The dry strength of oaks spiraling from the earth in contorted rhythms told of deep roots, stubborn and firm. Like locks of hair they emanated the powerful magnetism of the body-earth that bore them in defiance of the drought. There must be some rich blood flowing deep down to bear the rigidity of trees—sycamores, redwoods, massive oaks. Rich blood, rich humus, golden wheat, golden poppies, golden fruits, gold, gold and yellow sun, steady and strong where the kiss of the sea does not moisten with fog the parched skin of the land.

She went down the coast virescent with spring.

Because she liked freedom she bought a small car.

Breathing deep the rain, one with the soil, imbibing with fervor the gift of water, she zigzagged through valleys and hills drinking

18

freedom and sun like one reborn. She rolled herself upon the grass; her body gave in love to the vast breasts of the earth, to the deep womb of canyons rounded in expectation of seeds. The air was soft with flowers, pungent with orange-whiteness. It flowed through the crisp leaves of the oaks like woman-hair through millions of combs. It flowed through her, kissed her legs bared to the caress, kissed her browning flesh offered to the sun through dawns of sun ecstasy. It glowed in her eyes, staring at the light. She was drunken with mimosa, drunken with radiant orchards, drunken with fertility and rain, her body ploughed with passionate languors.

In freedom she roamed for weeks along the great ocean.

Then she reached the city of glamorous screen-fame.

Because she was young, agile, and beautiful, she was told she should have no difficulty in piercing through the host of potential stars starving through weary ordeals, and would be singled out. She took rooms in a studio club filled with youthful cravings and hectic pursuits. She found soon that women with beautiful bodies and easy characters were many, a common fare for men who retained the absolute power of casting or pushing one through the illogical steps to motion picture fame. She waited for hours and hours in crowded offices with mobs staring at some small window whence would come signs of possible favor. She had to disrobe to the weary eyes—yet never too weary—of casting officials in search of tempting curves for oriental screen-orgies. She saw in their looks the appraising of connoisseurs feeling skin and muscle, evaluating also the boon of easy-gained nights.

She had reached "screenland," modern slave market.

At first she laughed it off, bewildered yet amused.

She was too proud really to mind the banal desire of all-powerful bosses. Small pride only fears being insulted by small men. She looked back with ironic scorn and politely joked with them, as with misbehaving children. The whole show seemed such a farce that she could extract but humor out of the amazing scenes that came before her every day. She was eager to know all life, to sink her own vibrating soul as a sounding line into all depths, even though filth might cling to it and weigh it down for long miseries. It was all mankind, the living pulse of passion; not to dismiss, but to understand. How could one understand unless one would live through, if not with the muscles, at least with knowing looks?

And so she went through it all, bewildered yet amused.

But soon a strange disgust began to creep in her.

It was a slack time when she reached movieland. Thousands of "extras" were crowding outside gates, running credit accounts if lucky, or nearly starving; contented, if they were brave, with sunbaths and meals snatched here and there. She found it hard to get an entry to the sanctuary of the huge hangars, factories of dreams, temples of deception. Weeks of long waiting passed; endless procession to studio gates, or afternoons mobbed in narrow halls facing one door through which the chosen ones would disappear, often sacrifices to the strange Moloch of the soulless industry; soulless because of its world fame, because men and women were rushing in with dreams from all over the earth, hundreds competing for every little bit, all fitted just as well for the easy work. How could choice be made save on grounds of personal preferment, which meant lust or drink, or the gambling away of this or that?

And slowly, insidiously, disgust seeped into her.

passionate spring

But money was scarce and she had to keep on.

She could laugh at insults and ward off banal greed; but the drawn out, depressing routine of days reaching nowhere made her life rebel in helpless anger. Helpless, for there was no one to be angry at; no one but a machine, but the grinding of unorganized wills flaring excitement into emptiness or polite refusals worse than insults: "Nothing today! Nothing today!" The dull refrain, ending long errands from mountain to sea over miles of roads, far and wide roads to many a Gethsemane. "Nothing today! Nothing today!"

But money was scarce and she had to keep on.

She made many friends, women and men.

A strange comradeship there was between these many-raced faces gathered at the foot of the hills, browning there with the rainless summer. She was kind but distant; and most were kind but distant. Mornings, as she would rush in her car to some studio beyond the hills, she would pick up on the roads straggling pieces of humanity waiting, moneyless, counting on good luck for a ride. They stood on corners with tortured eyes, anxious for the passing of minutes which might mean being last and a failure. The word would come that beards were needed; and files of hirsute faces, as from a world long past, would flock on the trail to five dollar checks, ten dollars perhaps for the lucky . . . living in many cases on a week's, even a couple of days' work a month.

She made many friends, kind yet distant.

One had to be kind.

One could never know when some strange trick of luck might not transform long-drawn features, peering through casting windows from the outer world, into the powerful boss glancing through some windows from the inner world dispensing salvation. But one had to be distant; for who knew what thief and polluted one might not glare behind sad countenance, heartrending misery, arousing pity, or the composure of evening-dressed gentlemen wearing moustaches like coats of arms heavy with ancestors. It was all a huge, heartless gamble, bitter contest and ferocious struggle most of the time—all weapons free to slander favored ones, or to drag some director from the body of a long-beloved.

One had to be distant.

At last she got her first break.

After nearly naked ordeals in front of high-ups—"Turn around! Head up! Bend your back! Dance! . . . Hum! not so bad! Good skin. . . Will register well. Breasts a little thin. Oh! well, it will do. . ."—she was selected for a "bit" in a big Arabian picture to be made on location. She was to be the favorite slave attending the queen. Her clothes she could hold between two fingers; small trunk and some pearl strings. She was signed up. One hundred a week and free board in the camp, somewhere in the dunes.

That was her first break.

Weeks of "location" work.

Broiling sun beating on a camp with hundreds of tents, small and large. Work starting at daybreak in cold chilly air moist with sea-fog. Gulping hot coffee and banal fare, after cold nights and colder awakenings before dawn. Then hours of waiting practically naked on the sand which but slowly warmed up to the touch of the sun; then orders, counter-orders, confusion. Beasts and men

passionate spring

herded into masses, swayed by contradictory whistles, thrown into panic, to and fro. With the zenith sun, dancing would start. Hours of dancing, swirling, dropping, perspiration on the sizzling sand. "Once more! Once more!" slashed weary muscles again and again. Exhausted, scorched; yet going on once more . . . once more.

Weeks of "location" work.

Weeks of steady, cruel work.

She had to dance under the lash of some huge black figure, some tragic mimic of despair. The man was kind but awkward. He was afraid to hit. The director got mad. "Darn you! Can't you use a lash!" The man lost his head. "Picture!" The camera ground. He used the lash. She nearly fell, her breasts cut; but she was reckless, she went on. The assistant yelled, "Hey! Go easy! You fool!" The man did not hear. He lashed. She danced; she danced; her teeth clenched; she danced—until she fell fainting, bleeding. It was a good shot. They had made the man drunk to make it more real.

Weeks of cruel, relentless work.

The director thought she was game.

He went to her and helped her up. She opened her eyes enough to see his face agleam with sadistic grinning. He stared at her. He could not do much now before the mob; but she understood. They gave her a day of rest and treated her well. One senses soon when favor falls upon one from on high. One must be very kind then, very kind. For the favorite may either crush or grace from her bed of pleasure. Other girls laughed and sneered: they were jealous. He was hard to please. His pleasure meant fame. They must watch her and begin to slander her, carefully though—most carefully.

The director thought she was game.

He told her so plainly when location ended.

He asked her to come to his office. He was very kind. He inquired about past and family. He played at fatherly tones, essayed a few silly gestures. She laughed. She knew she could not do it. He was domineering and cruel. She felt his craving like some foul animal twisting round her limbs. She could barely breathe. He had almost hypnotic power. He tried to seize her. She flung herself back and with cutting words threw him away to his desk. He sneered like a beast. "Proud, hey! Well, you know, better not play with me . . . dangerous game here." She asked to leave. He frowned, rushed to her, almost crushed her both hands. "Now girl! Don't be such a damned fool! What do you want? A house, car, jewels? All right . . . but, by God!" She looked at him slowly, up and down, shrugged her shoulders and simply said, "I am not for sale, that's all." He burst out in cramped laughter and let her go. "All right! Go your own damned way, little idiot. But you hear, no monkey-talk and not one step of yours back in this studio; or else. . ." and the gesture that ended was harsh and cutting like a curse.

In this manner "location" work ended.

As she went through the waiting room a man followed her.

Face flushed and a somber anger in her eyes, she did not see him. He was an old man, had played the high priest in the lashing scene. When she was outside the gates, something broke within her. She bit her lips, clenched her fists, not to let go. But when she came to her car, she dropped on the wheel and sobbed. She was startled as she felt a kind hand pressing her arm and a voice saying: "That's all right, girl! Don't take it so bad. He didn't kill you after all. You aren't the first one. That's the game. Don't mind it." She looked at a smiling face shaking with fatherly pity; she remembered him. He knew. He had seen her come in and out of the boss's sanctuary. He knew. Her face told. She tried to smile too, grinned only and cried bitterly in his arms.

The old man who followed her was kind

He took the wheel and drove her to the beach.

They lay on the cooling sands watching the withdrawal of light and the slow rise of the fog, the cold, heavy breath of the compassionate sea moving earthward to mother the leaves and wipe the dust off their scorched eyes. There was a long silence. She was quiet now, looking far and away, following the motion of some things of the sea swaying on the big waves curling and breaking with the back power of great infinitudes. He looked at her distantly, as if she had no name, but were some transparent symbol of sorrow to be cared for, lest it might vanish and leave the earth empty, meaningless. He was dreaming through her at life; and it felt good to the wounded one, for that was quiet, silence, selflessness.

He lay near her for hours upon the beach.

Then she looked at him, whimsically.

The thing was absorbed now. It had struck and hurt. Now the time had come to shake off the ugly dream and live again more knowingly in the strength of one's soul, intangible. She fixed with a long clear look his restful countenance, a face long past middle age which must have suffered and forborne, and perhaps forgotten. His eyes did not shrink. They were deep grey lakes with soul-mist rising from old memories of sorrow. They were kind, full of acceptance, shadowed by some intangible dream almost beyond life.

She looked at him and laughed.

And gaily he also began to laugh.

Like two big children, they laughed at life, at themselves, at all the foolish water, tear-wasted throughout the ages. "What do you think he did to me?" she asked. "Don't know," he shrugged off. "I guess he might do anything. But the way you looked, I rather think he hadn't it easy!" and he smiled. "Easy!" she retorted. "Not on your life! I don't care, old man. I am not a silly girl to waste tears on my body, taken or not. You know what hurt? . . ." No, he did not know. "His eyes. They were awful. They pierced and tore me. It was ghastly. My body, what's the difference? He might just as well have had it, as long as he would get thrills out of it. It might have done him good. Men are such strange animals. But I couldn't bear his eyes. Anything, but not that."

His face was grave now. He understood.

She was a strange girl.

He had not yet seen anyone like her. Obviously she had known much of life otherwise she could not have this freedom and peace of a turned-loose self, whose moorings suffering must have burned, ere it could rise from the old fears and the old restraints —yet remain a self, unmovable and real beyond the tricks of flesh. He wouldn't question her. She might tell of her own accord. He had respect for all depths, this kind man whose eyes were heavy with soul-mist from memories of sorrow. He began to feel a deep tenderness for the lean creature whose heart was beating with a rhythm unfrequent among the herd of bodies called women,

passionate spring

lowing for food or for love. Old memories he had thought vanished lifted their heads to watch the new life-throb moving on from within toward the stranger.

She was a rare, mysterious girl.

She suddenly felt hungry.

They hurried back to Hollywood, growing proudly her first skyline, as a youth his moustache. Adolescent, easy, tense, inert, excited and unreal . . . indeed an adolescent youth in love with love and movement, amazingly self-conscious, innocently depraved and foolishly aping vices which cause no thrill but soothe the rush of blood from head to sex. The Boulevard was gay, rouging its facades with neon lights. Musso-Frank was recovering from rush hour and late players coming in, grumbling at directors who dragged on the scenes and kept one hungry and weary, in sheer obstinacy over some business which meant nothing. Rania and her new friend sat in a booth and ate the good fare, interrupted by passing "Hellos!" and open, lovely faces looking in, amused and gay. The evening poured into them—the rich, fragrant California evening, softened with fog, yet warm with the glowing of the earth that sun had so well loved.

Hunger appeased, they went on riding.

Over the high ridge above the lake they sat.

Under the moving fog glowing from below, thousands of lights were dancing. In long lines they shone, brightly marking the main boulevard, fainter ones for the cross-streets. All the south was scintillating; and north, along the San Fernando Valley, new cities were rising, coruscating the dark combs of mountains! Desert winds blew from afar, warm and soft, vast tender arms to relax into and taste of love, soft pungent fragrance like chrysanthemums. Men were children, mad, selfish children. They made love; they could never *be* love and silence and repose in the beloved—vast, endless repose from the weariness of self. Rich nights, never forgotten, the real live hours of California, when the sun had waned and the earth breathes perfume, and men might be beautiful and smile in love and repose. . . .

The hills were moaning under the winds, like flutes.

He asked her to let him be her friend.

He could help her along a great deal in the studios. He had worked many years for types; he had written successful plays years ago, cheap things he cleverly put together. Then he grew disgusted with the game. He had enemies who blocked his way. For a while he acted on the stage; then his health broke down: weak lungs followed a pneumonia taken foolishly in the madness of some broken love. Just a banal story. But somehow he had seen through it and won. He had lived in the desert; he had still a cabin on the Mojave Desert where he retired when studios got on his nerves. He had been five years in Hollywood; had seen the little churches go and the eucalyptuses, and tall buildings grow that broke the sloping of the hills. He had seen men of all nations flock by trainful to sunshine and moving shadows. He could have made much money perhaps, but cared little. He had just enough to be free, if needed, and live in the desert whose bareness and silence are kind to one who had suffered. He worked when good bits came. He did not know much perhaps, but had forgotten much. Is it not what one has forgotten that makes one wise?

He knew at least one thing—how to be a friend.

And so their friendship grew, strong and loving.

passionate spring

Some people smiled; others openly said the usual ugly things. But they were happy. He brought her to casting directors whom he knew well. With the few hundreds she had earned in location she bought lovely gowns, made others. She was ready for the game. Her strong features and big eyes registered well. She fitted exotic scenes. French and Russian sequences saw her running, from queen to beggar. Much of the dreary waiting in casting offices was over. She found enough work to keep her going without harassing assistants and directors for personal help; and the strange captivation of this unreal life began to possess her. . .

With her old friend, Johan, she found happiness.

It was a quiet, beautiful happiness.

For the first time in her life she felt a rich, unobstructive affection surrounding her. She yielded to its warmth as to the soft air of sweet-scented nights. He was gentle and full of humorous anecdotes. He had seen and traveled much. He had a keen sense of people, intuition of their inmost self, much respect and much patience. He was with her almost every evening when they worked in the day, often went for long rides, perhaps camped under trees, on the desert. He was patient and simple. He knew he was old and none too strong. He did not care to force his love upon her. He was waiting, dreaming often of her loveliness, of the supple body he watched dancing and running on sloping hills. He never asked her anything. She was happy, he knew. What did it matter? She might feel some day the need for his arms yet strong enough to press her as a lover and stir her young body. . . But he was willing to wait, not to spoil the rich comradeship, the quiet, beautiful happiness.

He lived in a small canyon toward the north.

A young, reckless friend of his, Richard Newell, had built the bungalow. It had several rooms, live fireplaces with updancing flames, a library filled with books, and solitude under huge trees—eucalyptus spears smelling fresh, rose-wigged pepper trees comforting in their stolidness. The grounds were left wild, still hairy with sage and darting yuccas. The soil was black, pungent with shed leaves. It rose rapidly as the slope of the hills joined in rounded embrace, two firm thighs vibrant with earth-love. A few goats were roaming under dark bushes, relics of old days. An old Italian kept them nearby. Rania loved them, drank their tasty milk. It awakened memories of her mountain-youth in Karpathian wilds.

It was a small, hidden canyon toward the north.

Richard Newell had left a year before.

His father was a wealthy man; his passion: oil. He roamed over the earth hunting oil, digging for oil, smelling oil. He was tall and lean, an old derrick sullied by the hell-born flow. He loved the game of adventure in strange lands. An Englishman, he worked with the diplomatic service of his country, and bribed and stole and killed to uncover the viscous thing that clung to his bones. Richard inherited from him a strange wanderlust and a violent nature, hardly tempered by softer mother-strains. He loved big deeds and crushing passions. Intensely selfish, he adorned himself with proud gestures whose glamor haloed him. He had fought in the air in Arabia. His tales were glorious, were true. He could do anything . . . and undo anything. His soul was of a condottiere; his body strong, nervous and irresistible. He knew it. He used it. Suddenly weary with Hollywood, he disappeared toward Asia. He had not been heard of since.

Richard Newell had left a year before.

passionate spring

The library was filled with books.

There were books of travel, books of adventure, books of science, books of philosophy. His dead mother, abandoned by his father, was a great reader, trying to forget and understand. She had traveled in the Orient and brought back in her soul the quest for silence and infinitude of the ancient races. Chinese, Hindu, Persian poets and lovers, mystics and sages, she read; hoping to reweave the rug of scattered memories with the many threads of wisdom. She left her books to Richard, who cared little, but kept them, partly because of being drawn from within to their mystery, partly to show off depth to impressionable conquests. Johan loved to read; he read aloud to Rania listening in wonder, asking big questions—unanswered yet, but stirring on, arousing, shattering also.

The library was filled with books.

She became feverish with knowledge-thirst.

She brought books with her on every set where she was working. She stole away from the yawping group of extras, away from improvised bridge parties behind scenery between director's whistles. She was tired with the constant aimless chattering of long days of illusion, in gilded costumes, tawdry gowns or rags. Adventures, love affairs, little scandals, tips for this or that . . . she knew them all. She became careless of comradeship, she hid in corners far from the lens, striving not to come into close-ups, letting ambitious ones fight for "getting in" near the star, indolent; but devouring books, books, more books. They laughed at her. Assistant directors chided her, rebuked and menaced. Distantly she obeyed, performed hackneyed gestures—"being French" with foolishly stereotyped demeanor to please Mr. X, who had been in Paris and "knew it all"; "being Russian" with languid, exotic pallor and blackened pupils; "being full of pep" with squirming contortions and shallow grinning. It was business. It had to be done. So little registered; who cared anyway? She was far and beyond.

She was feverish with knowledge-thirst.

She read all the books about Eastern lands.

She read travel stories. She dug into philosophy with passionate intensity. She began to grasp inner meanings she had never fathomed. She saw that the old visions and dreams she had nearly forgotten had been real experiences, vestiges or forebodings. She pondered over, dissected, compared, played with ideas, as with lives she loved. In her fervor, she sank into them; with her enthusiasm, they glowed, as huge diamonds dazzling upon soul-fingers. She read evenings, nights. She could not tear herself from the library. Johan, smiling at her new passion, suggested she might as well stay for good in his house, as long as she hardly ever slept in her own clubroom. She looked at him, straightforward, with clear soul. She knew he loved her. She was grateful. She bowed her head, smiled a little, whimsically, a little weary perhaps. Then she faced him with open love and joyousness. "All right, Johan! Friends always? As before?" "Of course," he answered.

Her soul had been caught in the dream of the East.

But it was too much for her body.

Hardly sleeping in spite of her friend's admonitions, tense over printed pages, strained in weary self-questioning, tired out by the routine work, long standing and waiting of the studios, her strength gave out toward the spring, and she fell ill with flu. Johan nursed her devotedly through days of fever and long convalescence. He was not well himself, and every cold he got roused again the old lung trouble never quite cured. But he was happy. She was sweet and tender like a young child resting in mother-love. She felt secure. She was drawing in fresh things that were life from the very threshold of a possible death. It was strange how illness would open up great fields of light, as if her strong body had been shutting them out by the glamor of health. She would not awaken. She would sleep long hours peopled with dreams and beautiful faces—dark faces of power like those she had seen years ago, and at times a curious shadow, the features of a man, indistinct, yet somehow spreading darkness and sorrow.

It had been too much for her body.

But summer and sunbaths gave her rebirth.

Climbing slowly up the canyons in the places of darkness of the hills, she bared her body and gave it to the light. And light took her and made her a thing of its realms, brown and glowing like warm fruits, ripe pineapples, growing from the soil amidst darting yuccas, bodyguard of speared watchers.

The sun was rich and stirring.

The sun beat forcefully on the place of darkness of the hills, on the place of darkness of the flesh. It was too much to bear alone, this potent sun, craving extension, inrush and possession.

The sun was strong and fierce. The sun would take one and melt one, and soft, lucent nights would follow with hot winds that creep beneath white sheets, that open windows, doors, and love gates. And amidst the fervor of the dry earth crackling with sun power, she drew, supple and warm into Johan's arms, that knew strength once more and rhythm and glory. Life flew in her,

33

sun-born, sage-scented, where the hills meet like firm thighs in the place of darkness beloved on the sun; and it made her well.

—∞◇∞—

CHAPTER III

Many months passed by with indolence, with sameness. Rania was growing into womanhood, rounding with maturity angular corners of body and soul. She was flowing into the quiet rhythm of a life in which the rippling of wavelets of excitement born of studio mock-storms was alternating with the quasi-seclusion of the canyon house, rich with loving-kindness and soul-stirring books. She had quieted down the pace of her reading, allowing life to pour and personalities to reach through her distant pride into her heart. She began to draw herself out toward human beings, no longer fearful of impacts, but eager to give. For she had found wealth that was indestructible and she saw men wearily dragging with spiritual poverty, hollowing out their looks—youthful, lovely looks of children, of beautiful soulless bodies.

City of soulless bodies, of pure instinct and receptive sensibilities. It seemed like a fresh moist clay craving for the sculptor's hands. And the hands joyously would mold and shape, unheeding the sticky matter clinging to nails and fingers. The night passed. At dawn the clay had dried up and there was nothing left but a heap of sand, ever-virgin sand, ever-soiled, ever-throbbing, ever-lusting . . . yet ever-virgin. For virginity ceases only when mind awakens from within—even be it but instinctual mind; and Rania was staring at beautiful bodies, unlighted windows of some dark rooms, limbo of unborn selves.

"Oh my poor unborn!" she would sigh to Johan. "I feel them begging me to mother them into being real men. They cling to me, they beat me in my womb of soul. I am willing, Johan . . . should I not be? But what is the use? What is the use! . . ."

He was willing, too. He had brought no chain to bind her to their happiness. Their happiness was free, with but few shadows of race feelings that were old and outworn to stir nervous tensions soon absorbed. She was free to go as she felt the urge. If destiny called for her service, she should answer.

Johan lived with the poise of one who had known destiny. He had seen the heights of what men call success; he had loved and won and withdrawn, for he felt it was not worthwhile. As he had called upon the higher, outer failure answered—as it so often must. Failure and pain he accepted as part of the game. Perhaps he had nothing to offer. But what matters "nothing"? He had himself to offer; his life, to make noble and strong and peaceful. And he went through, his grey eyes veiled to concentrate better on birth within. She had come to him, as some one always comes when destiny is ripe. He accepted happiness as he had accepted failure. He would accept whatever would be next, as he accepted happiness.

The year was still a slack one; much distress prevailed among the extras flocking in hordes ever increasing to the magic gates of the slave market. Drastic steps had to be used to stem the tide and the pressure of hungry looks and of willing bodies upon already satiated offices. Wages went down. Production being cut, the fewer the openings. Yet now and then sensational rises stimulated the hopes or cravings of always new recruits.

Rania was known and could easily get usual jobs. Johan found it harder, but somehow kept going. Often they improvised picnics in the hills, excuses to feed empty stomachs and legs weary of endless stations following long walks from corner to corner of the ever-widening studio districts. Boys and girls came, some with nothing but beauty, others with some vague craving for adventure, for reaching beyond. Hollywood—center of a world of unreality! Its glamor sucked youths from all races into its ever-shifting core, its poignant emptiness. It was no longer the little village kind and hospitable, filled with communal care, getting together and the like; and not yet a unit—a city—ensouled with a purpose. Here and there some dreamer would start a little "salon." For a few weeks few kindred souls would come and talk, escape from the rut of cranking cameras. Then friends would bring friends. Drinks would move on; radio twitter and squeak. And the "salon" ended in a fair, or a bored and sinless brothel.

Yet there was a strange uncouth fascination in this empty and soul-shattering existence with no tomorrow, with no chance of planning anything, always on the go or waiting, waiting to go, hanging on the phone day after day, hours of faithful presence near the dismal receiver, hoping for a studio call toward six o'clock, then calling to make sure one is not forgotten. "Nothing today. Sorry. Call again—in a week." Politeness, strained affability of casting offices worn to utmost irritability by endlessly ringing phones, by questions, by inquiries for jobs, by interruptions, schedules changed, directors' whims, lack of organization, waste, utter waste of time, money, lives. One wondered how they could keep on the grinning smile. Often they did not, of course. And curses flew and beastly treatment. Men, women herded like cattle;

no consideration, no attention, no sense of human worth. Merely moving bodies to fit costumes on. "How many uniforms left?"

"Ten."

"Damn you! Speed up and get ten men in the streets." There were hundreds of men waiting for the ten costumes. Five bucks a day—but many, many empty foodless days between the luck of fitting into costumes, and being herded around in the wet, blood-freezing draught of winter stages, in the suffocating heat of dozens of arc lights focused between walls upon which the fierce sun beat all day.

Yet there was a fascination, a strange disappointment when not called for next day set. One felt a dim jealousy for whomsoever rose to the thankless if well-paid task of sweating and grinning in the terrific glare and heat of spots beating you in the face—while camera grinds, director sweats, and again and again the same scene done over, tears once more, laughter once more; a silly, aimless, devastating sequence of harsh strain and empty hours of vague chattering, or bridge playing when the crew was not tough on the game.

It was all so unnatural, so unreal. Not like the theater, a few hours every night of plays reaching climax in front of responsive audience; but every day the putting on of illusion, the whole day the dragging on into tinsel costumes through backless sceneries, in strange company, doing awkward gestures supposedly real. It ate into your blood. It sapped your moral strength. You went down to the level rhythm, vaguely stimulated by an atmosphere of excited boredom and meaningless sex craving. God! One had to do something to stand it all, month after month. If faking be, then faking all along the line; in and out the sets. Freedom and restraint alternated. Mixture of reticence—one must keep a reputation—and of complete breaking down for favors from the "masters," or for the mere filling of one's own emptiness.

Yet a lovely illusion of spontaneity, of charm; life of bodies, of young, strong, muscular flesh, always in motion, always going —anywhere, nowhere—but going, riding, playing, shouting; couples everywhere, alive, sunburnt; sense of mating, of rhythm—broken, hectic rhythm, but dance all the same—and the endless hope that, out of this chaos, the one, the expected, might surge and meet you with this same freedom and this same dance, where there is no class, no tradition, no prejudice, where one starves today, tomorrow makes merry, climbs and falls—huge gamble, life gambling, strip poker, body poker, soul poker, chaos, madness; but going, going, on, madly on, on.

—∞◇∞—

There were big sets in the air and extras were pulling wires to get the many "bits" promised, expected, dreamt. Superpicture of the Thousand and One Nights. Extravagance. Gold costumes. Elephants. Camels. Mobs. Lots of excitement. Studio buzzing madly. Hammers. Curses. Hair-tearing. Rush of worn-out faces from office to office. Pandemonium. The greatest picture ever made!

Rania interviewed, waited, interviewed some more. "Come again. No time. We have not the continuity yet. For God's sake! Let us breathe. Sure, promised; next week. Call us."

For once it came through. She got a part, a real one. And she had not slept with the director, or kissed the assistant, or given booze to the wardrobe! Marvelous. Johan too had a part as a monk, dervish or whatnot. She was a slave turning into a bad princess who seduced the son of the hero and caused everything to go wrong.

Rania felt suddenly like a kid, being drawn into the mad vortex of days of costuming, tests, wig-making and the like. She forgot everything and was going to have a good time. Dance rehearsals. The first sequence was a grand orgy a la motion picture. Naked girls whirling vehemently and swooning into the arms of sedulous princes breathing heavily in big robes, gold-heavied and stiff. It was glorious.

After a week of steady dancing, muscles aching and feet bleeding under the strain, the dancer's group was ready. Rania was the second best. There was a star dancer; but the prince obviously would not have her, was to rush to Rania instead, drag her before the throne, and order her to dance; and then his heart would be lost and the next thing she would know, she would be a princess.

All inspired, though freezing—winter dampness made unheated dressing rooms breeding places for colds—the dancers, ankles tinkling, hair excited into feverish curls, skin darkened, nails reddened, with the utmost brevity of clothes thought advisable, came onto the huge set. Massive columns, gold draperies, bejeweled throne, black varnished floor from which assistants cursed away too-curious extras, completed the paraphernalia of Hollywood-bred Oriental splendor. Around the floor were colossal cushions on which some hundred gentlemen with grand mien, false beards and rubescent clothes were trying to stabilize with dignity their preposterous and warlike appendages. A couple of braziers were burning in a corner of the big high-roofed stage. The girls flocked to them shivering in coats they dared not keep close to their skin, the browning of which was not yet very dry. Yellings, whistle, shutting, opening of spotlights, heavy smell of floor varnish, of ether-pasting wigs and moustaches on rebellious faces, fumes of slow burning coal in the braziers. Heavy eyes half asleep still; too much love, perhaps! Hands stiff with quick rides in open cars from suburbs. And over it all the queer tension of something about to happen, of something being made; not really with the world public in mind, but as a thing in itself, self-sufficient in its unreality.

"On the set! Everybody on the set!" Latecomers push through, while assistants run, scold, drag here, drag there, scream, curse counter-orders, listen for the loudspeaker echoing through the din, scanning the directors' whims and ever-changing commands. The orchestra tunes in. The show is on; while the small one-eyed cameras record with blank faces the momentous events of the scene which will set millions of hearts and sexes athrill through five continents, which will set some to kill perhaps, others to quarrel with a banal wife, youngsters to mate hiding in corners; all because of the dream, the insistent dream, repeated endlessly, theater after theater, hour after hour to onflowing herds of wasteful minds craving release from meaningless jobs.

"Camera!" The dance is on—whirling flesh, dazzling scarves, fake jewels, shimmering lights. Men's faces glow on. A few twitter. Warmth increases, of perspiring nude bodies, of movement, of riveted eyes following arms, legs, supple torsos bending, twisting, offering themselves, near, very near, coming, gliding. Arms undulate, hands call, smiles glitter from lovely faces, dark, blue eyes, rouged lips. Paroxysm of the dance. The glorious bodies are to be seized, to be thrown, panting from the dance, into one's arms, over one's knees. One must kiss almost the moist flesh, kiss the lips . . . not too much, not too much; it is not in the game of extras, only for close-ups. Yet kiss the lips, be very real, very convincing.

The director shouts: "Warm it up, boys! Be yourself. Now let go.

Throw them away." And bodies are thrown away; but bodies remember, are hot. Acting? Oh yes, of course, it's all a fake. But flesh plus flesh is never entirely fake. And when the climax comes, when the girls rushing, whirling down some huge stairs are to be grabbed, fought for, carried away, with torn clothing and hot, convincing gestures, there are many who do not entirely fake, who fight a little too hard for the throbbing prey, who crave a little less fake, a little more real, whose blood must be restrained now of course, but is kept feverish and that night *must* rage forth with pent up power.

Somehow Rania at first fell into the arms of a dark-eyed man who looked suspiciously Hindu. Somehow she liked him and arranged to fall again at the same spot, as many, many times the passionate scene was re-enacted. During shots there were moments to rest in these arms which had grabbed her, to relax on these cushions, huge and soft, where the male body had dragged her. Words were better than silence. Conversation ensued. The man had a strange, powerful face. It was not fake; real brown skin, real long hair. She wondered, questioned. He laughed with big white teeth. He did not answer; but looked at her long. She became uneasy, near withdrawing.

"You, beautiful, strong girl," he said slowly, with a marked accent. "This is no place for you. You belong to the old, old countries, my country. They don't understand you."

She looked at him, puzzled, inquiring.

"Yes, of course, they will love you and you will think it must be so, because you are young, your body is young. But the real you is old, so old. It is lovely, very lovely. I can feel it lovely. All old beings are lovely; for young ones cannot understand why they are so quiet, and know so much."

passionate spring

Whistle. "Camera!" She had hurried away, troubled. The rest of the day she had to play her action with the prince who snatched her away and forced her to dance. She danced, eyed by the crowd; gazed at by friends and enemies, desired, envied, an image to be kept for long solitary nights for some not favored with love, a thing of beauty, selflessly moving, warmed by the primal urge of her own dark-skinned race that wandered over lands and struck no roots; race of free beings, of vehement loves.

At lunch hour she watched for the Asiatic with the strange knowledge of her. But could not find him in the rush that followed the words of release. Before going home, she looked again. He saw her, smiled and waved his hand from afar. She came home, uneasy and sullen.

—

The next day and the day that followed she saw him, the Asiatic. His dark eyes clung to her, piercing her beyond the flesh, rousing strange unbodily fires, longings for deeds of power.

He talked to her; deep, metallic, harsh voice. "You do not belong here. You are not of this puny race. You are strong. They are children, silly little children; just tearing through their easy dreams with no aim, gesticulating like madmen.

"In my land there are still some who know. There are secrets which give power. I shall teach you. Why waste your life doing foolish gestures, when you can be a god, command the gods and have nature your servant?

"I knew you as soon as I saw your body move. You have rhythm and will. I shall teach you how to breathe for power, how to still your wandering thoughts, how to rouse the Great Mother in you, the fire that makes one master.

"We shall work both as one. There will be more power. Life is like a battery. We need two poles for the spark. With the spark in us, we shall see through the wall. There are forces everywhere. All is alive. All these lives we can master, if we have knowledge and power.

"I have knowledge. I have studied ancient books. My father was one of a brotherhood in Nepal. He taught me. There are huge monasteries deep in the rock. They light fires that burn you, but make you god. Don't be afraid. There is no danger if you are strong. Only the fools fail, soft-headed, soft-hearted fools. They cannot keep their desires. But we shall not waste power, just to be like animals. Power which one keeps; out of that, one rises and masters.

"I don't want your love. What is love! Mock bubbles of dreams, dead before they begin. I want you immortal, a power. I need you as you need me. Together, we can have power, if we forget this race of fools, this suckling West, and go back to our old knowledge, our old secrets, our old strong nerves that do not collapse under shadows of pain.

"You love strength. I know. Of course not silly muscle strength soon turned over to worms. But strength that keeps, that grows stronger through centuries, free from the body. Body is but an instrument, a dynamo. Just a form to focus and release energy. When it is worn out, we get another one. But *we*, we need not go down and forget.

"Come out of these silly passions and silly loving, strong one! I shall show you the way. We shall leave these bodies and work, unseen. I know great men who will welcome you, too. Our old mountains will welcome you. They will uplift you. Cease bewailing the weakness of the mob-selves squirming around in this mock world. You want heroes, noble men to live a life glorious and free. You won't find them here.

"But in Asia, there are many. They are too great to let themselves be known and become prey to idle curiosity. What do they care about being known, when the world within, when all the powers of nature are theirs? But they work, be sure! They command; the fools obey, not knowing even that they are led from within their own brains. Will you stay a fool or be master?"

To become a master of life. To gain power. To live the hidden life of one for whom the outer show of man is worthy but of scorn, for whom the world of energy, form-controlling, is real, is known, is dominated. Oh! She was so weary of puny selves, of aimless chattering, foolish sentimentality and neurotic yearnings without strength. She was weary of this constant disrupting strain, of this ceaseless agitation without purpose, without concentration, without heroism and nobility. She was craving life real and dangerous, life that exalts, that dares, life of deep confrontations, face to face with the powers she knew were lurking beyond, powers she could only dimly sense, yet felt one with in intensity and stoic grandeur.

She was tired of happiness; she loved her old Johan dearly. But his very calm and peace was too quiet a pool for her windblown self raised in the vast abysses of life. Her Gypsy, Mongol blood was crying out for Asia, for immensities to sweep clean at the frantic pace of horses that had fire. She dreamt of huge mountains, endless steppes. She saw herself galloping through, breaking through this world into the other, claiming new tumultuous oceans to sail across, unchartered voyaging to unknown mastery.

The dark strength of these big, unmoved eyes fascinated her. She did not desire the man, though she felt his body rigid and steel-like, a tense yet strangely relaxed source of power. She did not love him; but she must follow him. This was the call for a greater life that could not be dismissed, that could not be delayed, that surged from within as a torrid electric tide when she was near him and he touched her back. It surged from her loins and rose along the spine, shiver of desireless yearning, reaching up, up, almost bursting toward the head. Powerful stillness, expectation of mystery, regulated breathing that produced a sense of not-being, yet intense energy, controlled strain—like steam speeding on joltlessly the huge monsters that tear along glittering steel.

They met as often as work permitted in his small cottage up in Laurel Canyon. A couple of tough, creepy oaks, Hydralike, rose spiraling up the earth. The wooden house was gripped into their iron tentacles, resisting, glaring with silk-curtained windows; a fireplace, a couple of divans, a few red and green draperies, printed scarves, cushions. He cooked strong curry. She loved it. It burned through. It made the breath dry and hot. He made black heavy coffee out of long-handled ibziks, boiled in the open fire. He had pungent, spicy incenses, benzoin, galbanum, and many strange-named ones which he mixed and burned, till the air was like a hot fog, dizzying and intoxicating.

He sat near her, gazed fixedly at her. She must still her thoughts, fix some dark spot, train her nerves, be rigid yet relaxed. He would touch certain spots of her body. And fire would seem to burn through her. Sometimes she would stay all night. They would not sleep. The world had gone out of consciousness almost. At daybreak he would take her, half-faint under the nervous stress and strain, to the top of the canyon. He would massage her limbs and make her breathe slowly, rhythmically; a subtle, uncanny life-stream would pour through her. She would feel relaxed and vigorous. She would hurry through the day's work as if she had slept long hours.

Johan was distressed by her new life. Not only she refused herself to him, to save her life power she said—he would have accepted that—but she seemed to fade away from him into a realm of mystery which, he sensed, would certainly mean eventual disaster. He had read books dealing with many types of Yoga; his friend, Richard Newell, had told him about curious encounters he had had in India, about fakirs, adepts and priests using many-sided powers to charm, heal . . . or kill. He was also acquainted with European writings on so-called occultism and had had experiences in Paris with a group dabbling in ceremonial magic; a group from which he escaped in time to avert the fate of most of its members, who met tragic deaths which he could not help considering as fateful sequences to the practices indulged in.

Rania truly looked more beautiful than ever with her eyes deepened by a kind of inner glow, her cheeks somewhat emaciated and a provocative air of intense jubilation as if intoxicated with powerful visions. But this very glow frightened him. He had seen it in consumptives when, at the threshold of death, life seems to brim over the cup of a translucent body. He had seen it once in an ecstatic nun who went insane with holy visions of saints and angels. Old-blooded Hindus might stand it and reach beyond; but could Rania, in spite of her strength, resist the hollowing from within, the burning of an energy, no longer normally spent, but volatilized and, under forced draught, hissing and flaring to the brain?

He advised her gently, calmly; begged her to be wary and probe the motive back of it all. Why did she want power? Why this frantic desire to transcend the normal boundaries of her race-body? Was it real spirituality? He opened books she loved, read to her from the

Bhagavad Gita, from the calm, quiescent wisdom of the Tao. But she confronted him with many arguments he could not well answer. She quoted many texts proving that powers need be acquired, that concentration practices were necessary for spiritual development. How could one hope to reach supermanhood before the powers of the body were transmuted, the animal mastered, and the Fire raised, opener of the great world where regenerated men live and work.

Her destiny had come. Characteristic indeed, that it should have been in the midst of the mob illusion of a wild set. But did not heaven and hell react the one upon the other; and would not the highest bound up from the deepest, as if powered by some mystic springboard? He did not need to be afraid. Their friendship and love need not be altered, because she was being reborn into a greater world. She would love him from some deeper and vaster recess of her heart as she would grow into her richer self. He was old and wise enough not to cling to dream bubbles and bodily lure, to transcend the personal into the impersonal, and love her into universal life.

But he shook his head and could not answer.

—∞◇∞—

Long strained weeks went by.

The Oriental film was slow in the making. Rania's part was lasting all through, with periods of rest, alternating with feverish all-day-and-night sessions in hot then cold stages—outdoors under the blatant sun blindly focused on one's body by means of huge reflectors, indoors under the pitiless convergence of burning lights—then freezing hours of rest wrapped in fur coats around stoves, lashed by draughts making the perspiring, dance-weary body shiver.

Johan, too, was working almost constantly, a fantastic part requiring the utmost of exertion, long night vigils, almost acrobatic feats, acting with lions and panthers strange to stand by, with queer steady eyes laughing at you, devouring you, scorning from the noble depth of untamable power.

Long strained weeks of mad illusion.

The spring rains had come, bursting open flowers over the hills.

The spring rains had come, swelling wide-bedded arroyos, whirling streams of power cataracting through unaccustomed sands and willow-haired banks. They had come with torrential strength, that year. Streets were flooded, Johan's canyon was torn by tumultuous waters. The house was nearly surrounded by moving mud, thick, brownish clay clinging to the feet. The road to his canyon was practically blocked by washouts. The studios were islands emerging from swirling pools. Extras could not reach their work. Stagehands, assistants, directors cursed and roared, in dripping clothes. Every roof leaked. Life itself leaked from every frame. Blood seemed to have turned into water, seeping mournfully through the skin ashen with grey skies.

The rains poured for weeks into swollen canyons.

It had been a tense, hectic day. She had worked constantly. Nerves were high-pitched. Everything went wrong. She had to stage a frantic scene of tears over the body of her dead lover. She couldn't do it at first. She was bored, sullen. She acted like a machine. The director scolded, insulted her. Everyone's will was pressing against her. "Cry, girl! Cry! You are mad! Your lover is dead. Break down

girl! Break down!" She couldn't do it. The director shook her. By
God! She would cry! He pinched her so hard blood came on her
arm. She screamed. Someone gave her whiskey. She was shaking.
"Camera!" The dead body. She bites her lips. Tears stream as her
face twitches convulsively. She cries. She cries. "Again! Once
more! More movement. Tear your clothes, your hair!" Her arms
beat the air. Broken, she falls, prostrated, lifeless. "Good shot!"

Good shot . . . good shot.

She is carried away. Her body quivers, nerves and fever. Johan is
called. He rushed her in his car, unconscious, to the house, across
dark stream and molten earth. A physician. Just nervous
exhaustion. Nothing but rest, complete rest.

From the roofs, drops fall unceasingly into a big tub; leaks, leaks,
everywhere. Drop after drop, like mad gonging; drops upon the
skull, beating, fever-mad, torturing. "Please stop it! Stop it!" He
piles up rags under the leaks to mufflle the sound. She is hot and
tense, delirious. He spends nights watching. A friend comes when
he has to go to studio work. Days, he stands up in the rain; nights,
he watches the curled body aching with strange pains.

With strange pains. . . Nerves seem to twirl in repressed spasms
all along the limbs. If she could only stretch, stretch! He massages
the warm body. She clings with her hands to the bed posts. He
pulls her feet. Stretch! Stretch! Something is locked, twisted that
cannot unwind. The body groans. There is fire that cannot flame,
fire smoldering, turned into acid corroding the vitals.

Shooting pains, sharp and rhythmic, lacerate the back of the loins.
They seem to pulse and rise from where the spine ends, flashes of
blinding fire, bone-rending. They shoot at the heart, contracting,
writhing under the mad inrush of power. Rigid face! Cataleptic.

passionate spring

Stretched eyes, dry and glaring, like desert stones torrid with sun. The lips twirl and twist, pitiful. "Oh! rest . . . rest . . . to forget, forever to forget."

The body groans. It howls pain. It bends, it curls, it breaks, exhausted, powerless to shake off the mad demon that ravages, that consumes.

Johan stands up, worn out by work and vigil, staring at her torture, staring. Awesome silence creeps into the room as she relaxes, as she forgets. Huge black faces seem to sneer in the dark, seem to scorn and call for the prey; huge black hands to claw the panting flesh. Confrontation. Who shall win? He or they? His will is tense, tense, like steel cables harboring through the storm an airship to its mast. Someone must win. He or they? Oh! for power, power to cast out the torturing hell—to carry her on, blessed, into the sun, into the silent sun, far into the desert, where stones are kind, peaceful, wondrously nonhuman, strainless and warm!

Someone must win. Someone must suffer. Someone must die, perhaps. It is the law, the great, mysterious law, that calls. Will he accept? Can he accept? He is an old man. What does it matter to love, to compassionate love? His life had been sort of failure—outer life. But who knows victory? Is failure victory?

His life opens up, a lightning flash through the black silence. Confrontation. Rania's body groans. Torrid pains tear up again. "Johan! Johan!" Poor, helpless voice! She knows. She has played the mad game. It is hurled back. Aroused power is pitiless. It devours. It sneers at fool's pride. Promethean pygmies craving fire! Now the curse falls, the thunderbolt. It rages forth. Shall it be stayed? Can it be stayed?

Johan rises. He accepts. Let the fire burn! And in the black silence hammered by the rain, his naked flesh took her writhing body and quenched the fire that struck at his own heart.

She recovered. Something had been released. The body lay unnerved. Strange weariness, poignant, void. Automatic motions of heart and lungs. Food entering, chemically scattered into molecules, indrawn, dispersed where needed most. Waste leaving the body. And the circuit again, aimless, strange to behold for a soul that wandered beyond the pale of earth-stars and was called back.

It is home again now—confusion, wonderment. It is all quite dark yet—an intricate web of life-streams, red, yellow, black, gold, which flow into one another, yet separate; each necessary, integral, with its own rhythm and its own meaning. But one cannot grasp well. The soul is still blind from the awesome dark, the torrid darkness of beyond the earth-stars. Familiar things stare at you as witnesses to some great expiation. Familiar things are mysterious judges. They confront the soul from a depth of knowledge which men do not possess. On them, destiny writes. The soul cannot help reading, though it may shrink, though it may sob bitterly, as if it had all been in vain, in vain.

Is there ever anything in vain?

Days of recovery, of silence.

Johan went on with his work until the picture's end. He began to cough. He was so weary he could hardly move. His emaciated feverish flesh seemed to stick around him like wet clothes. A sad, faraway look dreamed from the depth of orbits caving under some heavy load. As soon as they were free from work they left for his cabin in the Mojave desert. The physician had listened to Johan's lungs. The wounded tissues within the lungs were tormented again by the destructive powers. They had never entirely recovered from past assaults. Now suddenly the evil had struck deep; there was little hope left of recovery.

They rode to the desert, where stones are kind, where strange cacti—like semaphore arms—signal frigidly to the stars the passionate woes of men.

—∞◇∞—

CHAPTER IV

Late spring in the high desert.

The sands paint themselves up to seduce the sun. Soon, under the
torrid love, the face of the desert will lose its roses and purples and
grow thin and dusty, in long summer weariness. But now the few
sprinklings of rain have wrought florescent wonders. The winds
that blow from north and west have still the cool taste of snow on
their breath—fresh, strong, clear air that makes the skin lucent and
stirs effervescence in the lightened blood. Rubescent skies dome
evenings of peace after days of work or riding. It is good to
breathe. Stars scintillate, bejeweling the pallid horizon scissored by
mountains. One thinks of infinitude. Deeper breaths lift one up.
The sky shrinks into one's eyes. Dizziness of beyond. Rolling over
the still tepid earth, the sand dribbles into one's clothes. Away
with them! Rapt in darkness, the passionate body breathes, loved
by myriad-tongued winds.

Late spring in the high desert.

passionate spring

Rania and Johan, alone.

A small wooden cabin and long dreams. Much to be pondered over; much which the heart dares not utter in loud words, yet broods over. Long wonderings through the sullen stillness of nights. The older body was very ill, would never be well again; the younger, strong, fervent, radiant with recovery. But the souls—mysterious, unknown; of what strange dreaming, watching, pondering was made their silence?

She nursed him, carefully, tenderly, guiltily; surrounded him with loving-kindness. She looked at him from within some hidden recognition as if the all-important thing could not be told, yet was hovering, hawklike, over the field of live moments to be snatched away into some dark recess of the night of soul.

Rania and Johan alone.

She was restless, filled with the unexpressed.

They rented a horse. She went for long wild rides, saddleless, her strong thighs mastering the raw will of the beast. They flew centaurlike, toward the dry ridges, sharp teeth of defiance baring the fury of the fabulous being with four-footed speed and two-armed power. Then alone against the rocks, black and grey with bleeding veins of metallic ore, she sang. Deep, resonant voice with strained intonations and tones powerful with soul-craving fervor.

She was restless, bursting with songs unsung.

She sang to the desert.

Songs never-written, songs clamored from the life urge, melodies strange with unWestern steps, with glissandos nurtured by Asiatic ecstasy. She was calling for the new races of men, summoning from the deep of unearthly motherhood the god-born heroes of a richer earth. Sands and rocks seemed to swirl to the rhythm of the songs—dust tone-molded into shapes of power. She was straining her soul into the future. Would the fierce dawn break? Power was still burning into her blood-soul. Fate-battered, she was still the rebel, once more stirred by the magnificence of stones.

That was her desert song.

Johan listened to it in wonder.

He could not fully understand this Amazon power. His life was flowing with quieter rhythm, ebbing away now in the burnt offering. Soon he would die. It was well. He had done his work. In a way somewhat dark which he could hardly fathom, he had saved a soul he loved. He had put himself between her and the powers aroused to destruction. They struck at him and he collapsed. And now the freed one was singing, singing, songs vibrant with infinitude, songs hard and raw with elemental strength, magic with powers he could not face. What did it all mean? Songs of triumph born of his own dying? Songs of liberation? Some nights they would soften and caress; his heart would sob away with childlike despair. At dawns they would burst forth with the sun rays. They met the noons like bells clanging, deep-throated, for masses of light as for a ritual never-ending. Rania's songs surrounded him who was dying, and life poured in from very far, unearthly: from what planet, her home?

Johan listened, listened in wonder.

To escape summer heat they drove north.

passionate spring

Through fir-lined ridges, chasms of torn granite, deserts to the right, fruit-laden orchards to the left, they reached Yosemite. High up where one faces the vast display of slate-colored masses towering into glaciers, with precipices gaping, thirsting mouths of stones streaked with foaming rivulets and cataract-thunder, high and clear into the love of skies, they dwelt, souls dilated with infinitude. The awesome silence of mile-deep canyons stilled Rania's songs. She felt a yearning to draw on paper the monumental masses, to extract from the rocks and capture with blacks and whites the thousand faces that stared at her from some heroic past.

Great heroic past of this rugged North!

From sequoias to granite!

The still-beating pulse of titanic ages, when men, beasts, and trees grew up with the insolent strength of elemental youth! Now the earth was old, contented with small parturitions. Then she must have loved fervently some fiercer sun into the birth of those huge lives; red-blooded trees with angular arms, shivaic idols dancing regal rhythms; grey mountains torn by inexorable glaciers, white lava pouring from celestial volcanoes to fulfill the curses of gods.

From sequoias to granite!

She drew them all.

In harsh, cutting strokes she sketched the monstrous shapes, enlivening dead forms into myriads of faces, re-enacting the mystery of creation. The pulse of slow-heaving stones stirred dark masses into consummation of ecstasies that were hardly of the earth. She had captured the elements' dances. Then she would pin the sheets on the log walls, cry triumphantly to Johan to come and see the new birth. More often than not on the next day she would tear them into bits and throw them into the abyss, laughing, a priestess feeding the eternal Moloch with limbs of tortured children. And fire invisible would spout from the monster and seize her and force her to draw again new prodigious scenes of cosmic mysteries.

For weeks and weeks, she drew.

Johan's life nearly sank away.

It was too strong, too vehement perhaps this life, this presence of fire burning near him with lionlike tenderness. But he did not care. He was to see it through. As this was the end, he would rather take it gallantly and speed it up into freedom for her. Their money, accumulated during highly paid weeks of studio work would not last forever. They had bought a new car. He would use it to surround his death with speed and new horizons, across mountains and deserts, wanderers feeding on the glorious body of this land of power. So they went back to the desert, and after a few weeks of rest during which he seemed to recover wonderfully, they left for inland canyons, painted deserts and the throbbing rhythms of Indian tom-toms.

Johan's life was ebbing away.

She knew it, but as one who has come back from death.

Death had no terror for her, nor did it arouse any sentimental gushing. It had to be faced, as everything had to be faced. The important thing was to make the most of life, for we meet death with the same strength wherewith we, everyday, are meeting life. Being filled with life she was indifferent to keeping it safe, away

passionate spring

from the thieving of death. Her indifference of strength met his indifference of repose. They both knew. Everything was clear and firm between them. Her love was too deep to surround him with a shut-in and invalid death. She rode him to his death with the adventurous joy of lovers escaping toward a new life. How could one fear who had met death and won?

The willing victim too wins immortality.

—∞◇∞—

Tom-toms beat still in the rock-hearts of stalwart Redmen

through ridges and mesas pungent with brown earth

and green foliage of pinyon trees.

Tom-toms and feet pound silence and soil

fecundating the dumb into the living,

magic forces of will stamping the inert

into the magnificence of corn-growing rain.

Tom-toms beat still in the dark of nights

cold with altitude clear and electric.

If war no longer summons the loud bangs

that once have roused the brave for the battle;

if the Redman has lost his eagle diadems

and parades helplessly for the white shadows;

if trains cut and darken the rigid canyons

chiseled by strokes of divine hammers

where men that knew commanded the thunder

and roused cornbread out of stones;

if children and adults desecrate their past

with the piteous worship of Christian idols;

yet the land of strong men is still power

that beats upon the soil that is daring and strong,

and the earth is still red, blood-bearing and rugged,

and canyons resonate under sun and storms

with the massive fierceness of crystallized thunder.

Huge world-spine bearing strong-spined men,

we may yet discover the mighty currents

that stream up your loins

from pole to pole and from man to god!

Men may know some day the mysterious forces

passionate spring

that make from within the Redmen hard, stoic

through the long communion with the soul of the land,

with the silent awe of men that face power.

Huge world-spine, living fire that may blaze forth

under the magic call of a race of heroes—

great canyons between vertebrae where the force escapes,

torrents that tear vehemently through vitals

of the giant body of the continent—

immense spaces where man knows his measure,

is born god against the vast indifference of the earth. . . .

Tom-toms beat still, rugged and raw,

calling, calling yet from within, the race of heroes

who shall tame the mounts and bear them seeds,

transcendent seeds of regenerate manhood.

—oo◇oo—

Rania lived in the exhilaration of that male power which confronts at every step the traveler across the great plateaux. She drank it in with awe, yet jubilation. It was so strong, she was often stunned by the immensity of the experience. The earth opened to her and she experienced the earth. She realized there as never before that great elemental body on which men crawl in soul-intoxicated madness to be more than men. She knew the earth; she knew the stone; she knew it in her body, in strange mystic possessions. The tom-toms beat birth into her, and the rain that fell at the call of the iron feet trampling the sod for endless hours tore through her body in great cataracts of life. She ceased thinking. She lived deeper than thoughts, where the unconscious meets the earth and is made again in its likeness: a rich, hard matrix teeming with unborn. The chants of the brown throats echoed in her own heart. She heard the strident, wild tones of the Navajos, the deeper sun-born melodies of the Zunis, the magic chants of white-robed Taos men who guard jealously the mystery of the sacred mountain where rites take place, hoary with earth-magic.

One day a storm advanced fiercely upon them as they rode through a mesa. The road went uphill and down a number of small arroyos, dry save when the rain would thunder through, rolling huge stones like children's marbles. It came with incredible suddenness. They were riding slowly watching amazing clouds piling up purples over darkened rims. Midway across the arroyo they heard a big crashing noise. Unwary, they stopped. In a second, torrents of water had rolled by the car a foot deep, heavied with mud and stones. The car refused to start. The water streamed up into the engine. They crawled against the wild stream, bruised by stones, wet to the bone. The rain began: a downpour. Johan, who had been bearing bravely against the corrosion of death, fell exhausted, shivering in dripping clothes, fever mounting high while awful coughings shattered his beaten frame. There was little to be done. The car stood in the stream, half under water. No blanket. No dry clothing. Rania decided to walk along the unknown road hoping for a nearby house, fearful as she was to leave Johan alone. After an hour she reached a small Indian pueblo and managed to get some men and a cart to follow her down the road to rescue Johan.

He was breathing heavily, with great pains, coughing blood. They carried him to the pueblo, laid him on rugs near a fire. Strange, dark, impassible faces looked on, surrounding the two whites. Heavy silence broken by the spasms of the dying body. Someone went for a doctor. He lived far. Nothing to do but to try and ease the fading away of life. An old woman made some sort of a plaster which seemed to relieve the pain. The breathing became heavy but more peaceful. The night passed. At dawn the doctor came. It was hopeless. He could but soothe the burning flesh.

Dark, quiet faces looked on as Johan opened his eyes and tried to smile at Rania holding his hands firmly—black, strong eyes, weary of stone-immensities, ravined features ploughed by sun, wind and rain. He, now lying in death-fever, fire mounting up his body to sear the grey substance where the cell multitudes are mastered into the single will of body; she, bent over his body as if to shield it from some power of destruction. Vaguely it recalled to the dying memory that other scene in the little canyon, with the rain also beating against windows, gurgling along the walls; the girl burnt by the strange fire her recklessness had summoned, with dark faces he could sense watching for their prey. . . . He had willed it. It was well. Life streamed before him as he knew it, as he had found strength to live it, with youthful folly and mature acceptance, and the old smile of compassion and indifference. Destiny was rolling back. It had known itself as a human soul. It was free now to move in its realm of wholeness, synthesizing past into future, bringing its small wisdom-gift to the temple of Man, which aeons are building with such gifts as cement.

The body lay still near the fire. Near the fire all bodies have ever grown and died. But some dare enter the fire and be burned. The flame from below means death, for some; from above, rebirth.

Rania looked into the grey eyes in which the mist had risen to the fullness of their orb of vision. There was nothing more to be seen. But now because they were dark they shone like mirrors; and Rania saw herself in them.

She saw herself as she was in him. She saw the many threads of destiny that were he-and-she together. She sensed them as they stretched into far distant eras; she sensed them as they must weave themselves again into the future patterns of lives to come. She realized her debt to life which had been entered into his book of merits. She saw that there was no distinction; that all books were one, perpetually balanced. She sensed the completeness and changelessness of all, while separate selves make patterns, white and black.

She, too, was a maker of patterns. She knew how to make meanings out of whites and blacks. Would she have the power to make meanings also out of her own life-whites and blacks? Time opened. She saw a great figure print a few positives out of old negatives numbered in her book of past. She saw tragic blacks cloud the sensitive paper; streaks of passion, frenzy, huge shadows. The printer threw the paper away on the desk of life. Tomorrow it would appear, confront her. She shuddered a while. The dead body was quiet, restful. Above her an old squaw was looking on expressionlessly; little papooses, awed and silent, bundled up in a corner.

It was all real; all life.

It was well. An artist knows how to deal with shadows, how to lighten them with great glaring lights. She knew that in life's book accounts always balance. She breathed deeply; closed the eyes of the one who needed them no longer to stare at the false without, peopled by strange shadows and deceiving lights. She closed her own eyes. Life beat in her, calm and vast. There was no fear, no passion, no desire. It was all open, all ready for the confrontation, whatever it might be, to whatever path it would lead. For one moment, she forgot all, in the completeness of remembering all. She felt then that Johan's soul had finished the ultimate review from the grandstand of death. The mob of lives dispersed. The day was over. It was time for her to go. It was one more chapter closed. It was well.

Johan's body was buried deep down the mesa as he had wished. Rania left the battered car and rode in the fast train to Hollywood. He had willed her all he had. She returned to the house in the canyon. She was facing new life, alone.

—⚬—

She kept jealously alone.

She had decided to give a year to intense work, drawing, studying anatomy, technique, the history of art, fitting herself for creation. There was too much life in her not to create. It had to out-flow, else the body would burn in self-destruction. Power must be used, to build bodies, or selves, or magic forms, masses or tones. She felt overwhelmed by her own power. It coursed through her. It cried aloud, insistently, to be reckoned with, to be fed with more power. Often her body ached throughout, vitality pounding from within, dilating blood vessels, organs unused, swelling tide of imprisoned lives. Something had to be done. She was too proud for an easy release. She would dam in the flow and create from within, fashioner of shades and lights, arouser of visions that would carry outward the power to men.

She kept jealously alone.

The past was forgotten.

She had an incredible sense of forgetting the past. Her mind remembered, extracted meanings, drew comparisons, analyzed cycles and the rhythm of destiny. This past was all in the present; but the present was free of it, always virgin, like beaches made anew every dawn by tides, with the same freshness of immemorial beginnings. She was filled with her own living. Yet it was not selfishness, for she was thoroughly generous, considerate of others, sinking herself in souls encountered to feel their needs and give accordingly. She felt alive to all pains and all wants. Her motherhood longed to nurse poor aimless souls into warmth and love. She had no closed gates to keep away beggars. Her pride was of a more regal kind. It was the pride of one who *is* power and cannot help dispensing it; of one who *is* great horizon and cannot help encompassing all men in her light-gift. Not selfishness, but intense, overwhelming selfhood, concentrated energy flashing through a little channel—the soul—into a machine—the body—generating fire and power inexhaustible.

The past was forgotten.

But the present was not yet the eternal.

Her dynamic intensity shut her soul out from the repose of being destiny. After Johan's death, as something in her communed with the ultimate peace of death, she had sensed for a few moments the pure impersonal peace of the beyond of self, the poise of ever-balancing forces. But she could not recapture the calm, the childlike wonderment of the moment. Blood was singing too loudly in her ears songs of gestation and glorification. She would have to lose much blood, be broken up perhaps, battered by greater powers, ere she could forget present as well as past, and be eternity. Too much light in the life-drawing; more shadows were needed to rest the vision of the beholding soul and release deeper meanings, deeper rhythms, all absorbed now by the glaring whiteness of the molten life.

The present had to die into the eternal.

—∞◇∞—

CHAPTER V

Months passed of intense work.

Life was held captive by the strong grip of her will. It had to pull inward, to grow knowledge and mastery. But strong will is not strong against a deeper destiny. In will there is self; and only beyond self does the sea of destiny open, which is power and law rolling cyclically to restore endlessly ever-disturbed equilibrium. It was self in her that called for creation, for the throwing off of its plethoric wealth; self, the power that impels life into matter, that forces outward through the magic glamor of desire.

Months passed of studious work.

Richard Newell came back.

As Rania was drawing in strained fervor, the door opened and he entered. Seeing her, he stopped, apologized, and inquired after Johan. She told him the story of her comradeship with him, of his death. She asked when he would want her to move and to give him back the house, thanking him for all it had meant to her and to Johan. He looked at her, wondering, admiring. Oh! There was no hurry. He might not stay long in California. He could as well stay at the hotel. Was she living alone now? Was she an artist? Could he see more of her work? His voice was warm, metallic. His entire being vibrated as one who has dared much, lived much, forgotten much, who had seen many lands, frequented alien races. She remembered afterward he had struck her once as being, by blood and birth, a hunter, "a mighty hunter before the Lord." His body moved like an animal's, with inherent rhythm. It was a strong body, youthful, intensely male. A hunter.

Richard Newell came back.

He remained.

—∞◇∞—

Against such meetings no human force can claim the narrow will of its own selfhood. For the self is lost in the surge of blood which tears from the heart, washes out all dams, washes out all peace. The soul stands back aghast and wondering, unable to grasp any pattern as yet, any meaning in the downrush of the flood. The bird in the soul, freed, takes vast draughts of air, bends its wings upon the storm and rises above valleys and plains where houses are lit with quiescent fires. The dog in the soul howls, frantic to rouse the sleeping god. The tiger roves through the jungles of heat-tense body, clawing the wet humus with its electric thirst. The sage in the soul watches, feels the winds of destiny and smiles, studying the queer combustions of molecular humans.

They met with elemental richness. It was strong, intense, raw. In him there was no refinement, no subtlety. He was a hunter with terrific blood passions. He struck. There was nothing to be done, anymore than the earth could hide from the sun. She drank the sun. Her body vibrated to unknown feasts of life. It was beating into her with the insistent, precise, inescapable power of a huge sledgehammer. She had lost her body-self: it was all pelted into the furnace of the race-self demanding perpetuation. There was nothing left in her to resist. She had become the act. She had become sex; a partaker of cosmic infinities, of the unselved world of creative energy. With him she reflected life in its wholeness, in its parturient immensity. It was dissolution, then ecstasy, then life reborn—an assumption of power, perfectly harmonized blood, the race recreated, continued, triumphant.

There was triumph; yet, from afar, a vague, poignant sense of disaster. It was as if one had become identified with some volcanic element, had plunged into earth-caverns reaching to the very core of life; yet all the vast roar of flame and thunder suddenly blended into awful silence through which sighed the low whistling of sun-scented breezes moaning away—far, far above—for the departed Eurydice. In the magnificence of the many-limbed dance there came a moment when all life dissolved into a narrow little hollow, somewhere, everywhere. There, God must be found. But suddenly a great distress came, as if she no longer could desire God. The emptiness became excruciating; the hollow began to eat up all of her, weary, ever so weary. It spread all over her, till the heart ceased beating and she thought it was death. Then a great wind would blow from the rim, filling the cavity with liquid fire. The body would blaze forth, cling to strained muscles. And consciousness would stick to tiny little things, valueless, but magnified into importance, as to drowning men, floating wreckage is transformed into salvation.

When she was left alone she would try to think and evaluate. She would start back with some past experience, try comparison, opposition, the placing of the now into the pattern of the past completing its growth. But somehow the chain of events would rush off at some point in an inexplicable way. There was no causation, no sequence left. Something had happened which absorbed all past, because it had a glow of timelessness.

She was fulfilled, radiant—but silent, Richard at first had respected this silent aloofness, perhaps because he himself floated upon the same quiescent depth of repose, because intense rhythm had worn him out into negative response to her ecstasy. But he was of the hunter's race, never satiated with blood-fulfillment, a mad rover through forests of bodies straining fervent trunks and limbs to the sun. The trees answer possession of light with seeds. But what are seeds to the hunter? Only prey yet to be born.

He began pounding her with endless questions. "Are you happy? Why don't you speak? Am I boring you?"

She glowed into love, smiled, kissed him, fondled him like a mother. The male resents this mothering in his depth. It shields the home. The conquered woman turns back as a mother to draw him in, more and more in—to herself, to her warm quiescent hearth, to the unborn. The hunter rebels. It is then that brutality begins. He essays violence, cruelty, because he senses himself weak before the indrawing suction of the bewifed woman. Fighting with shivering heart, he loses his head and his temper. Jealousy, men call this. But it is the rancor of the male losing ground, of his blood-self fearful of being stretched into the family self, of being expanded beyond the obvious cycle of desire, tension and release.

The release never fully comes. Tension gnaws from within. While the woman dreams from the race depth, or listens to the waxing moans of her supernal self sighing under the stars, the male sours into distrust, ferments in the locked barrel of a haunted mind; orgasms turn into meaningless poundings, kniving back the soul staring helplessly.

Rania was soon aware of the strain. She thought of the usual remedy for this fear of indrawal in man; travel. She had become pregnant. To protect the future, she had asked marriage. She was Mrs. Newell now. It sounded strange, somewhat ghostlike. But she smiled it off, thinking of the one who was to come. They would have to travel, to have passports, to behave socially. She could not bear lying. She had met that destiny. Whatever it would mean, she was game and would fulfill it, until freed for greater tasks.

Thus they went, eastward. Once more, after many years, she visited the huge, blackened cities of the plains. She had groped through them, shadowed by her father's cravings or the common greed of music hall mobs. She was driving through a seeded earth with overbearing clouds that soon would turn into hurricanes. Some great life cycle was nearing completion. She had reached her twenty-seventh year.

—∞◇∞—

Paris.

Old world teeming with dead beautiful forms, with mental alertness and vivacity of speech and composure. Elegance born of long adaptation to social living, to the slowing pulse of racial blood turning into nerves. Nerve-subtleties, nerve-debauch, nerve-heroism, nerve-love. Old world feeding for centuries on polluted roots, built upon lies and crimes and the refusal to confront life save through the fallacious patterns of brain-born dogmatism. A feudal world in disguise, with motion picture castles dismantled, all facades; but with intellectual partitions and sophisticated ruthlessness. A world of autumnal splendor, with pungent leaves, now nearly shed, humus-making, softly sinking into alcoholic fermentations, into dream fabrics—under the lashing of winds and the drowning of endless rains washing clean the black trunks, patterns of beauty against velvet skies.

Paris.

A life growing within.

She wanted to surround this birth with all the wealth of past magnificences, so that, having absorbed this past while still in her, the child could start life as a striving toward a future which would grow normally out of such a prenatal assimilation. She wanted to make her blood rich with cultural atoms ingathered, filtered through the sieve of her discriminating mind. Profoundly, intently, she was synthesizing in her body a cycle of centuries into a unique moment of consciousness and rebirth. If there was life worth remembering in this past it should be gathered, molded into the form of a beginning. She stood as a living link between that which had been and that which might be. She offered her body and soul as a meeting ground for the past's ascent and the future's descent. She was conscious of great tensions, of accumulating power at each pole. Would the spark create the great noble human she had willed with all her passions?

A life growing within.

Against the life, hatred.

Richard hated that thing waxing in her. He hated it for her

withdrawal and her consecration to the seed. A deep resentment flared up in him as he touched the curving muscles doming the birth-to-be. He was no hierophant of hallowed mysteries, but one who sees, feels, touches and breaks into submission. A hunter. He craved her, because she refused herself. His looks gnawed into her body, tearing her aloofness, that he might make her clean of all but him, of all but his love embittered into nerve-rending passion.

He fed with alcohol his hatred.

Tense struggle between two wills.

He could hardly touch her without making her shiver as if burnt by strong acid. Dark desires beat upon her. She would resist, sneer at him, shame him with biting sarcasms. He would leave, helpless, pass away the night, drinking, drugged perhaps. The fever of the decadent city was eating into his nerves. He looked haggard. He wanted her; he wanted her. He would cry as a baby begging her. It would not hurt the thing. She loved him; she could see it was wrong; it would end wrong. He could not stand it. She stared at him, with contempt.

Tense struggle through long weeks.

Seventh month.

The child stirring. Another rhythm asserting, strange, helpless, irregular rhythm of a caged life which had known the vast expanses of solar fields. The little hollow contracting, moving with the dance of fists and feet, swaying, absorbing, quieting. Joy mixed with queer fright, with tense expectancy. Long brooding, dream-making, holding thoughts that might not mar the growth, trying to be calm, loving, compassionate; the alembic and the old alchemist watching the fluidic mass turn into strange shapes,

passionate spring

merging into humanhood.

Seventh month.

The storm struck.

He could not stand it. To know that the thing moved, that another rhythm was beating at this womb, he could not stand that. He went wild, menacing, his mind frantic with the sense of her, remote, absorbed in the unborn. Familiar things sneered at him. He would kill himself, make an end of this miserable farce. Then she could be alone with her child; alone, alone! A fool, forced to beg love, to beg men, to beg, to beg. . . . Enough of that! He was going. He slammed the door, tramped downstairs. Her blood froze. She felt him demented, blood crazy. She rushed after him. In the rain she called for a taxi, following his. The hunt, the hunt. . . . He stopped in front of a house. She caught him as he stepped in. "Richard! What are you doing? You are mad. You are mad! I will be good to you. Come back." He sneered. Ah!, now she was talking sense. But he was through, through. A woman had come. He asked for a room, whiskey, everything. Rania clung to him. He dragged her to the brothel room. He seized her wrists, he crushed them till she screamed, broken, sobbing. A great disgust, a great pity streamed over her. Useless, useless. Such ugliness, such poor, helpless misery! She looked at him with big, opened eyes, sad, very sad—pitying. He shuddered. A distorted look writhed through his face. He reeled away as if struck. Her body dropped, bent against a couch, flabby, unnerved. Something broke in him. Something sharp knived him through the heart. He groaned like a beaten beast, fell toward the door which burst open, and ran, ran . . . far away, far away.

The storm had struck.

A sharp pain roused her. The woman of the house was near the bed, anxiously watching. "What happened, dearie? Did he hurt you?" She was afraid of scandal. Rania understood. The pain in her womb increased. The shock had been too much. The thing had broken loose.

"Quick! To the hospital. . ." She clenched her fingers in supreme defiance. Perhaps it could be saved. She must be strong. She reached the hospital; she swooned upon the bed while the thing was born, faintly crying to useless life.

It was a girl; but she did not live long. A few weeks afterward, as normal birth should have occurred, it was all over. One dream more that crumbled, one more death, one more failure.

—∞◇∞—

Richard, after a day of mad raving, had found from the woman of the house where Rania had gone. He had attempted seeing her, but stubbornly she had refused. After a couple of weeks she had been well again but stayed near the little helpless contorted body, tense with the giving of life. After it had died and had become but a small imperceptible heap of ashes, she went back to the hotel where she lived with Richard, at a time when she felt quite certain of not finding him. She gathered quickly her clothes, books, jewels, money available and left on the table addressed to him an envelope containing the hospital bill with a few words: "This is for the birth and burial of your daughter, whom you killed. Good-bye." She had reserved by phone a few days before a cabin on a steamer. She caught a fast train to Cherbourg, boarded westward, arrived in New York and left after two days for Hollywood.

After discovering the letter and his wife's flight, Richard had gathered from information snatched from the hotel boys and from a diligent search in steamship offices Rania's boat. He cabled: "Am coming. Please wait for me at Plaza Hotel. Forgive me. Love." He cabled also to a private detective firm in New York to watch for her at the pier and follow her moves. As he reached the city a few days later, the detective informed him of her departure and destination. He hastened to the airfield and flew at full speed across the continent. He reached Hollywood a few hours before her, drove to their home, had it cleaned in a hurry, filled it with flowers, bought a Buick roadster and waited for her.

She did not come the first night. She rested at the Roosevelt Hotel as he soon learnt from the man shadowing her. But the next day she walked to the canyon. She hesitated a moment when she saw a car in the garage, but knocked at the door. Richard opened it. The room was warm with a huge burning fire, fragrant with roses and carnations. She stood amazed. She could not understand.

"You were waiting for me? How did you come here?"

He laughed jokingly. "Air mail of course. Does it not feel good to be home again?"

He wanted her to forget. He had his best manners; whimsical, childlike, cajoling. She did not speak; she did not smile. She had not expected he would dare to come back, not so soon. Her steel-colored eyes were filled with fog, huge icebergs melting from behind the pupil.

She might forgive, but how to forget? Crimes may be brushed aside; but a certain kind of moral ugliness cannot. As she stared at him, facing like a stone his forced eagerness to please and to be loved, his clear-cut features seemed to alter and swell into a lurid sneering face. A horrible twitch distorted the mouth that was outwardly speaking with baby tones as a naughty child begging the mother forgiveness. The eyes were shallow and half-closed, sick with covetousness.

She shuddered. She hid her face in her hands, convulsive. He stopped talking, frightened. He knelt near her, taking her arms in his hands that were moist, hot. She pushed him back. He wouldn't understand. He came closer, nearly touching her face. Oh!, again, the wolf's hunger! The beast snarling, writhing with brute hunger. Would she never be free, free from male bestiality, free and pure and clean, clean like snow, that snow which fell upon her mother's corpse, far away on the mountains, that fell upon her own strained body clinging desperately to the salvation of the tree, above the pack of beasts gorging themselves with flesh?

So vividly the past rose, that she seemed to hear the dying voice cry out to her, "Hold fast!! Have no fear . . . I am strong yet! Be brave, my love." And she saw the woman back against the tree, lashing furiously the wolves crowding in upon her, falling, legs half torn, yet lashing, lashing until a black monster jumped at her throat and stilled the mad courage of that soul.

And Rania violently sprang upon her feet, throwing off the body that clenched her limbs with repressed greed. She ran to the fire in front of which wood was piled. She snatched a long twig, another, another. Richard ran to her: "What are you doing?"

She laughed, insanely. "Show you what you are—a beast, a beast!"

She beat him over the shoulders, over the breast. A blood-fury took her.

His eyes dilated, aghast, enraged. "You are mad."

She cried with laughter. "Murderer! . . ."

passionate spring

He took her arms; she snatched herself away. She slashed him in the face. She beat him, until he stumbled, haggard, half-unconscious.

She stood, petrified, for a moment. Flames burned into her eyes like molten steel. She stood. She heard him groan, moan, like a hurt beast crawling to its lair. Sneering, she caught her coat and bag lying on a chair, opened the door jerkily, jumped into the car in the garage, and drove away.

Hearing the motor start roused Richard from his stupor. With bleeding face he rushed out. The detective who had watched Rania met him in a car.

"Shall I follow her, sir? She went up the pass in the Buick."

Richard glanced at the car, a Buick too. He laughed bitterly.

"Get out of here," he yelled, "I shall follow myself. Watch the house." And he sped madly toward Cahuenga Pass.

—∞◇∞—

Race in the night along the hot valley cooling with stars, along the sharp turns of the canyon up and down the ridge. Race through the thickening fog spreading its wet fume across the Ventura Valley . . , Santa Barbara. He thought he had seen the car, but was not sure. The streets were gaily lighted. He had to stop. He would try the coast route. A vague fateful instinct seemed to guide him, this road, that road. He stopped at several stations; they might have noticed her. He knew she would have to fill the tank soon after Santa Barbara. She might forget and be stalled. Or did she turn around and come back? He would try a little longer. He had been speeding; he should overtake her.

He asked once more at the station near San Luis Obispo. Yes, she had stopped; a girl with dark hair in a steel-colored Buick. She was all out of gas, had the tank filled and darted away at awful speed.

Race in the night. . . Blood had coagulated in his hair, stuck to the cap he had put on to hide it. He tried to pull it. A sharp pain tore through the skin. He swore; had to stop a moment. He was lame. The fool must be rushing over sixty an hour. He had lost time, asking people on the way. By God! He must catch her. No child now to go soft over. He had been taken aback when she struck him. Damned female! If he could only grab her, grab her pliant, resistant body! She would know this time. . .

Morning. He asks again. Yes, a car has been racing a while before; couldn't see who was in it. She must be aiming at San Francisco. On, on with the race. In front of him, dust swells. It must be she. The car refuses to go faster. King City. The long windy stretch. He is held back by some stupid truck blocking the road. Five minutes lost. He tramples the road, raging. The way is cleared. He charges on. This time it is the car. It has slowed down. Perhaps she is worn out.

She hears him or senses him. She looks back; and furious speed shatters again the steel monsters. He wants to stop her, passes her, yelling to her. She takes a sudden turn to the left and dashes on unheeding. Lost time. He follows her, on to Salinas, way past. Again he overtakes her. Will she not stop? He is afraid to bar the road. He must wait for some obstruction, for her to slow down. Thick rolling fog dampens the awesome ride. She must have steel nerves to go on at such a pace without rest. Big dunes, fields of artichokes; the Monterey Bay. He passes her, signals to stop. The road is wet, slippery; as he twists himself at the wheel he does not see a sharp turn; one wheel hits the sand, the others skid; the car bounces over, upturned lightning. The panting mass hits crosswise Rania's car which roars over, writhes up, collapses, a huge dead monster, into the sand.

When farmers who had heard the explosion of steel came, they found Rania lying with torn metal half-crushing her legs. The other car was on fire; later only a charred body was discovered under it.

Rania was taken to Monterey. The surgeon did his best to cope with an almost hopeless condition. The bones of hips and legs were broken into bits, even the lower vertebrae were hurt. There must have been inner contusions; a broken mass.

Yet she did not lose consciousness. She told her name, asked for Richard. They lied to her and said he was very severely wounded. She gave the address of her bank, of her lawyer. Another surgeon was summoned from San Francisco. They tried operation after operation. She was stretched on the bed, bound up tight. She could not move. She was but a big feverish knot of pain. They gave her morphine. But the pain merely went a little distance away. She could not sleep. She was very calm though, strangely lucid. She was dreaming, tensely, passionately dreaming. Some connection had broken somewhere within. She could not control her thoughts. She did not think, but dreamed endless, vivid, ecstatic dreams, as one dead. She dreamt of dancing, of wild movements against the winds, of swaying rhythms as of wings. It flowed through her, this rich, powerful dreaming, a cataract of waters shattered over broken boulders. She felt everything tearing apart in her body, a huge crumbled cliff. Pains, sharp and explosive, would burn through. They would come from afar, like thunder clouds, heavy, stirring; they madly burst forth into lightnings, excruciating. Perspiration would run down her forehead. She had to close her eyes. She could not move. The nurse would try and soothe her. A little morphine.

The nurse was a lovely woman, the daughter of Mrs. Falkner living in Carmel–a quiet, peace-loving woman devoted to the study of philosophy and ancient religions. After many unfortunate experiences mother and daughter had found shelter in a rustic cottage, reading, dreaming, though actively interested in all the new things coming into the small but intensely alive community. Hilda was nursing, on and off, to help her mother. She usually did not do it much at a stretch; but she had been impressed by the heroism of the poor broken girl whose soul she felt so strong and real, bearing the ordeal with stoic quietness, never complaining, smiling, even when tears of pain would roll over her rigid head cramped into immobility. She stood at Rania's side for weeks, for months.

Five operations were performed. But the fractures could hardly mend normally. They tried grafting bone. But in spite of all, it seemed impossible that she should ever walk again freely. Internal lesions had also caused much trouble and recovery might never be complete.

Months passed in absolute immobility. They ceased giving her morphine. Then the most terrible weeks began. The body–tense, struggling for action, for freedom–aching with the drug's desire. Not even the absorbing acuity of pain. No longer the steady flow of dreams. The soul bound again into the body, encased by bandages, by weights pulling the neck, the feet, pulling day after day, week after week, of caged life.

Mrs. Falkner came often to visit her, brought friends. Someone loaned a victrola with many records. The brave soul roused a rich, beautiful sympathy. Hilda would read to her for hours. Time ebbed away.

At last the doctors let her go, deciding nothing more could be done. Little by little, she learned to move again. The stone became vegetable. The vegetable grew aching legs that needed heavy crutches to begin again the weary conquest of space; huge crutches, ugly weight while the flesh sags and crawls, jerkily rises. It was pitiful. She would never be without them. She would never move much, nor bear any strain. The hurt had struck deep. It had knifed the vitals. The strong plethoric life had been broken, wasted. Now the will of soul would have to pull up and stretch the loose strings.

Rania's mind was clear. She saw the task. She was game. At first she laughed at it. But the laughter became strained and bitter. As she left the hospital and agreed to spend the first few months of recovery at Mrs. Falkner's home, as she began to face herself alive and free amid alive and free people, far from the subtle distortions of reality that cling to sickroom walls, a terrific reaction set in and blackness covered her, pall of bitter despair, of tortured rebellion.

—∞◇∞—

spiritual flowering

CHAPTER I

Strong men face strong crashes with bitterness or ecstasy. Bitterness claws the soul, vulture of unanswered "whys," black hunter hovering over moments frenzied by self-torment, shivering preys to the bird of doubt darting from the clouded mind. The sea has breathed thick rolling fog over rocks and cliffs. The foghorn ululates dull ravaging tones of death. They drop upon the brains they torture, rousing fever, implacable fever corroding the strength to bear the questioning of fate.

Why? oh, why?

Is it necessary that the body be racked, every bone be crushed before the caged embodied self may rise into freedom? Is it necessary that love decay into lust and the raving passion of males yoked to torment as unavoidably as death to body? Is it necessary that concentrated life burst asunder the frame containing its pressures and leave it a wreck on the sea of moments, helplessly swaying with the tides of fate?

Why? oh, why?

Rocks were groaning under the sea-blows. They stood, though, harshly cemented to the earth with molecular compacts that only milleniums had power to dissolve. Redwoods aimed with red sap-anger dark arrows at gods they heard laughing and spitting fire in the storm. The fire struck perhaps; yet the love of root and bark for the soil knew centuries of fervent possession. All lives seemed strong, ever widening, ever assertive, rich with significance and completion between the two valves of earth and sky. Was man only the pearl, a shining disease to bejewel some satanic feast beyond the Milky Ways, where dark nebulae hurl twisters of silence at life, sneering at its joys and its fulfillment?

Why? oh, why?

The rough grandeur of Carmel pounded upon the invalid—sledge-hammer of sea and silence upon her mind at white heat. The cleft tongues of Lobos snaked the sea, the wind hissing through its scale-like cypresses, dark and contorted. The earth grew medusas from every cliff point to petrify the stars which might venture to look through the cloak of fog, woven by the motherly love of the waters. But even these would surge and harrow, clench the coast moaning under the demented fingers of the waves, clench the brown throat of the many canyons, until every living thing would resound and groan, with shrieking sea gulls overtoning the wails. The summer months dragged endlessly, lost in grey dampness, cold fog, dull light. The cottage was closed in by four huge pines whose tears tapped the roof, ghostlike. Disheveled cypresses along the road muffled the insistent hollow rumble of the sea. Through their wildly stretched hair, one could see the sloping hills hesitate and disappear into the moving ocean. Up the valley the thinning grey gave promises of sun, beyond. It was poignantly beautiful, unreal. Rania lay down, shivering in the unusual dampness, wrapped in blankets, staring at birds wildly careening against the winds, screaming laughter and scorn at earth-glued humans and fools' agonies. Trampled wings, she; crushed under the iron mockery of this age. She had lost selfhood–save for violent denials, convulsions of a broken "I." She was humanity hurt and shattered, watching, scanning, despairing, bitter, falling back in stoic silence to the peace of the stone, yearning to unconsciousness . . . because stars were hidden and gangrene was gnawing the frames of things, and muscles no longer had the power to say "yes" by acting out the within.

Why? oh, why?

She realized that something deep, inescapable had happened to her life; the body-dirge was but a symbol; or had it been a parturition, a needed holocaust? Within too, the frame of her selfhood had been crushed. No one there to mend the gaping wound through which unselved humanity was pouring into consciousness. Dimly, slowly she began to feel a sense of being beyond her actual self, of being a lens through which immanent life was being focused into awareness. She felt a strange splitting of substance: a part of her becoming very hard, strong and transparent–a crystal whose peculiar shape was being polished carefully by unknown hands grinding with pain the convexities; then, the other part very soft, almost liquescent, a colloidal something which could absorb anything, which was to be open to everything, defenseless, the plasma of lives-to-be. At times she felt herself almost as a huge eye shaped by wills pressing like superphysical muscles. She was an eye confronting life . . . but unfinished, still being made, still lacking optic nerve and the power to interpret images from without.

Yet, images were being formed in her, back of the lens; images that men were making with their lives and relationships–strange, ugly patterns of artificiality and decay. These images burned her consciousness. She had suffered often before from the thoughts of human misery and abjection. Thoughts only; now the lens reflected the very vibration, the very intensity of it all. She felt disintegration creep into her and stench overwhelm her defenseless being. She could not resist: there was no "one" to resist in her. She had become a body: open, a great harbor filling with waste disgorged by steamers. The race was flowing into her; but these generations were of decay, rotting leaves of an ending vegetation. Fall had come. Rania knew herself as the earth damp with the rain, a bowl into which humus was being made out of the refuse of life.

The horror of it seemed unbearable. Underneath all the mock of our lives, the eye which she was X-rayed the alcoholic fermentation of death. Faces opened to her which she casually met; and hypocrisy, conceit, moral cancer, bared themselves. They glared at her; they preyed on her. She was defenseless. The eye would not close.

She could hardly walk. They drove her through the canyons; she touched tall, fervent trees; she lay over the rock warmed by fleeting sun-rents in the fog, or, deep inland, she rolled over seared meadows with the soil pungent like roast coffee. Frantically she wanted to move, to go, to go; but the eye would not close. It was inescapable.

Oh, to sleep long moldering stone-sleeps unaware of tides, of saplings pushing through, of swaying suns and moons... unaware of men, slime grown vertical, dropping lusts like poisonous seeds in the womb of life! Weariness, weariness of the hours and days avid with unbearable woe that was of no one and everyone, ubiquitous, protean woe that had to be breathed, tasted, made clean again perhaps... But how? By what mysterious tragic alchemy?

Reading. Of course, she was reading. But what was worthwhile? She tried novels, but heroes and heroines would become so real to her supersensitive faculties that she would suffer their agonies, yet laugh at their puny pleasures. With passion she would sink herself into human souls, and there had to see, had to remain, had to absorb. She craved loss of boundaries, loss of I, loss of all that men hold precious and holy. If she had been able, she would have walked in the wide streets of some huge city. She would have called to her all the sufferers, all the restless and unappeased. She would have held them tightly to her breast, close to her warmth . . . and given, given, given; till there were no more, no more, nothing more that was alone, that was yearning, that was burdened.

It would be horrible, yet so marvelous. Perhaps something might open somewhere, men might smile; perhaps the vertical ooze might vie with beautiful trees, fly like sea gulls, shatter with the thunder of young energy. Reading. . . There was little else left; that and drawing. Slash the white sheets with black scimitars; scar the virgin paper with outbursting frames, hurled masses and lights tearing through in unbearable radiance! When the sun was out, she would drive to Lobos or the farther cliffs and capture with quick motions the dark selves of cypresses and rock, the strained thighs of the hills hip-bathing into the sea. She would fling her breasts against the earth, sharp with cut straw, bare her breasts against the earth, and cry, "My earth! my earth! take me into thy nothing, into thy silence! I cannot bear it. It hollows me. It hurts me. It is burning me, your woe and your men's woe. Take me. I want to sleep. I want to sleep . . . forever."

The suffering burnt so deep she became almost insensitive. She was silent, staring at the farthermost, as if watching from a tower-top for a messenger. Mrs. Falkner, who had respected her strange moods and had attributed them to the purely physical tragedy of the accident and her wasted life, began to feel anxious. There was something unnatural in these blue wide-opened eyes that seemed never to close, that seemed to strike bottom in all things, even the most trivial. Her drawings, she thought, were on the verge of madness. They had a tragic fervor which seemed inhuman. They were epic with a passion that laughed at all shams and all littleness. They were cosmic dances disdainful of men.

But Rania was still very calm outwardly, very affable. Many friends would come to visit her. Conversations would run in Carmel fashion from seaweeds to personal problems, and household bothers to cosmic consciousness. Women came to her with their tortured selves begging for cure. A strange company of human beings! Men and women (mostly women) coming from everywhere; because, having lived, they wanted to settle to their death; because, dissatisfied and hurt by cities, they craved the shelter of pines and sands; because they needed silence to face issues or deface old structures of fate; because life being easy and cheap, needs lessened, one could afford being with oneself, independent of others, freed from job slavery; because earth and sea told their love in thrilling stanzas that poets and painters could capture and eternalize. Underneath all, they were drawn inescapably by the mysterious power that oozed out of the peninsula, that made the air and stones and trees tense with rugged will and excruciating selfhood, that drew one with the fateful pull of cosmic adjustment when destiny called for the marriage of Carmel and human soul; a strong catalytic, fateful conjugation.

To all these wanderers, analyzers, yearners, questioners, Rania afforded a strangely warm, yet distant indifference. Most felt richer and more alive when they left, yet in a curious way empty, with nothing to recall, nothing to lay hands on, no remembrances of her. She seemed intensely alive and yet "she" was never to be sensed. There were words spoken; words which slashed and whipped and hurt and brought light; words that one seemed to be saying to oneself. The strange girl, steel-eyed abyss, was nowhere to be found, nowhere to be touched.

Perhaps she would show a few of her drawings. Suddenly, from them, a terrific elemental being would stare at one, a being of incomprehensible passion and power. One would lift one's eyes and glance at the woman whose hands materialized such scenes and witness only the farness of bereavement, a baffling infinite unframed, unclosed, unthinged. Had the deep fog made her in its likeness?

Outside, in the chill of evening the foghorn ululated and moaned the death of horizon, wept for rocks and hills vanished, unselved into grey. Outside, the felted streets lay with magnified pines booing shadows at lost travelers through Carmel darkness. Outside, loveliness and mystery, along the coast scissored by passionate hands cutting a saw to sunder the earth. Strength and silence. Relentless vigor. And shadows of old disappeared races, gigantic manhood, that had wrenched from the gods Promethean fire.

—∞◇∞—

Mrs. Falkner's life had been a tragic one. Her husband drank and gambled, with money and lives. They lived in wealth. She had been educated as a society girl, from ball to ball; she disliked it, but as an only child she felt compelled to carry on the traditional routine which led her to an early marriage. Soon after, she began to feel that her husband's business was not all that it might be. She wondered, rebelled, implored him. He sneered at her prudery and old-fashioned honesty. She had a daughter. Duty bound her. He drank more, dared more. One day the police came to seize papers in the house safe. Jail faced the man. He chose suicide.

Her health broke down. She was prostrated for weeks. A friend had brought her books on New Thought. She read avidly. She had to reconstruct her world. It lay grinning death at her feet. For years, she felt a wound inside and as if her dead husband was breathing poisoned fumes into her; nearly every night, for years. The girl, Hilda, refused to marry. A boy who loved her enlisted out of despair and was killed while flying. She felt herself a murderess. No word was spoken about it.

The mother felt a change was necessary. They went west. Something opened in them as they crossed the mountains, as they saw the sun set in the waters. The New Thought seed grew. Mrs. Falkner began to devote herself to study. Her world was waxing strong again. The dreams suddenly stopped. She felt her husband was in some way released. At all events, she was freed. Hilda followed courses in Berkeley. Years passed. They discovered Carmel; it was the place. As with many others, the recognition had been immediate. They bought a cottage; books, radios, a few beautiful things of the Orient filled in the space of living, which became animated with a quiet, somewhat shut-in, activity.

To them Rania had come from her long months of immobile torture. Hilda loved her with a strange attachment that grew at times almost wildly, then somehow seemed to subside as if frightened by the clear emptiness of the invalid's being. How could one love transparent space? Rania knew; said nothing. She was infinitely grateful for the nurse's devotion. She loved the girl with her remote, translucid love. Hilda gazed at her often in silence; nothing said. Hilda turned pale: "Are you looking at me, Rania?"

"Well yes, don't you see?"

"Oh! no, not at me—somewhere, far, far through me. You frighten me. I feel sometimes a great face of jade, a goddess, is

spiritual flowering

standing back of your hair; and your face is but a little strange hole through which the goddess looks at me. She is beautiful, but so far, so far. . . ." Rania laughed. She would like to see the goddess! She would draw her. The following day Hilda was looking at some drawings Rania had made, when she exclaimed: "The goddess! Here, look, Rania—that really is the face I told you I could sense behind your head. Did you know it?" No, of course, she did not know. There was another face on the sheet also. A powerful man's visage of Oriental type with strong arched nose. Who was he? Rania had drawn both one morning, waking up. Dreams, perhaps . . . perhaps memory, recognition. It did not matter.

Nothing much mattered. After months of tense cruel sufferings as if harboring all the distress of man, a dull indifference had come again with jerks of bitterness and rebellion. What did it matter? She had brought death in her wake. She had been clawed by that same fatality. Well, that was the great play of life. Millions of redwood seeds are dropped, after spring and all the warmth and wealth of the earth have seemingly labored to bring forth those seeds. One here and there strikes roots; millions decay. The same hilarious waste everywhere, the same folly of gestation, struggle, race for the seed, seeding, waste, death, death, gestation—endless, endless wheel.

Men talked about it. She knew it. She had been it. She had sunk herself into it. The great eye had seen. The vision had hurt. It was all right. Pain does good. It keeps one beyond the image of selfhood. Flesh hurts also. Bone-breaking does not smother entirely the fire. The fire does strange deeds when the self is gone. It is all chaotic. It has no form. It leaps forth. It must carve an opening. It burns the walls of body—one body, then another. Oh! strange life-passion which corrodes, which rebels against fate, the queer fate of humans lost in paroxysms of pain and love, bitterness and ecstasy!

The great eye has closed. Rania's face, too, perhaps. It has become more self, less open. Hilda does not see the goddess behind the dark hair; the dark hair has unloosened. It is warm, like spring grass on the sun-matured hills. It flows upon one with the swift stir of the wind that fans the green fire, the bouncing, cracking flames of un-nuptial love.

Rania smiles, tenderly. Her hands are winged, impalpable motion of desire. Fog, fog—long weeks now, unceasing. One must be warmed and glow, where life blurs all things into greyishness. Hands may rouse colors, too, out of soft bodies. They draw, they sculpture the quivering resilience of the limbs. They make patterns. Bodies make patterns in the silent room trembling with excruciating tenderness.

—∞◇∞—

Gestures, many strange gestures we perform. It is queer how little we know the slope of our destiny. Our gestures run in canyons we never suspected. They become brooks. They dance to the sea. They are lost. A woman scans the distant breakers from one hilltop. They are not disturbed because the brooks dash jauntily to drink the shore sands and the bitter taste of the ocean.

Rania has become translucent again. The eye has opened and sinks his ray into the soul of a wounded girl. The goddess face is back again. Hilda stares helplessly. Was it a dream? Her eyes question. How can there be any answer? There is never any answer. Man is a strange being who never may answer. He often believes he does. He only thinks aloud. Gestures answer. Deeds. And no one can tell, only he who tastes of the quality of the deed, unrelated to memories or anticipations, unladen with potential regrets. Morals are subterfuges to capture deeds and pin them for display on corks of respectability.

Rania smiles, this morning. A warm wind has blown the fogs westward. The sun is strong. She smiles at Hilda, who rushes to the garden, fumbles about, pulling weeds, pushing stonelets to and fro—the young body that does not know love, that flushes with dear remembrances the soul dares not face.

"Hilda, you must grow stronger. You must grow vast and open like all great things of nature. You must not be afraid of your desire. It may be worthless, not your own, a starved craving of nerves which have no peace and feel here and there for the true tone that shall release the flame pent up within. You are still bound in a fear, bound in the experience of another. You came to me with the whole of you hurting your hands, so tensely it had rushed to the farthest of your nerves. You came with your desire trembling, yearning to be released. I am an open door to all living quests, Hilda. If the door has brought death to several who entered, it is not my task to bewail. I have acted freely from the roots of my nature. I have never forced my nature with mindborn phantasms. It has been fulfilled. Tragedy fulfilled it. It has pounded my bones; it has made me an invalid, unable to mother bodies into birth. I accept this as fulfillment; as I shall accept death, however tragic, as fulfillment. It may be useless. It is a bitter woe to think of uselessness. It has made me weary and craving the stone-peace sung by our Carmel poet. But I have no happiness, as he had. I am alone. That too, means fulfillment. So I have sunk myself into the mire of Man. I do not despise. I refuse not to love. Because I am alone. That showed me my nature. Yes, this aloneness, this broken body. It has shown me my nature, which is my destiny. I shall not withdraw... Do not look at me with tears. I have died too many times to weep any longer. You cry because you have not been born. You opened the gates of me to find yourself. Now you are afraid. I am not closing these gates. But I know that you will not come again, because you have found yourself. That is why you cry: not because of what we did, but because of what you have not yet been, because of your unfulfilled nature."

—∞◇∞—

spiritual flowering

CHAPTER II

A week later, Mrs. Fallkner told the news of the coming to Carmel of Boris Khsantianoff, a young philosopher and poet whom she had met during a flying trip south the year before and who had impressed her deeply. He had been holding classes in Los Angeles, had lectured up and down the coast, toured Canada and the eastern states and was coming to Carmel for a few weeks' rest. She had rented a cottage for him nearby and he was to have dinner with them and a few friends the following day.

Carmel had been hospitable that year to messengers of glad or sorrowful tidings. In the little miniature world wrapped in pine-sown fog with foaming fringes of sea, comets had been welcomed that dropped seeds of unborn cosmoi. Dancer, musician, poet, psychologist, orientalist, socialist, reformer, ironist, devotee of this or that European, Tibetan or Hindu master, one after one they had been drawn into the concentrated furnace of a community whose roots had wound themselves around rocks and trees, whose multifarious and highly individualistic, yet not individualized, consciousness seemed to call for fecundators. A refuge for women, children, artists and troubled souls in pangs of selfhood is bound to attract messengers and prophets—mental males. A miniature world: many seeds for one inchoate matrix—and as a result tensions, yet a rare sense of aloofness, of not bothering about others. Thus many small groups, many shrines made of cemented hearts, or companionate activities, much excitement, endless discussions, a passionate sincerity blending often with an equally passionate versatility. A soil in which souls struck roots and grew trunks of self, resinous and highly combustible pines, tortured, disheveled cypresses, red giants rust-eaten yet proud, and many small, hard, scented bushes hugging close the soil in fear of the sea winds.

Boris Khsantianoff came. The woods were washed clean from the summer; cottages freed from sight-seers and festive commercialism. The skies irradiated peace and the lucent fervor of the winter climate. Cold nights, warm sun, hills aglow with tumultuous viridity. The disconcerting Californian fall which is a subtly inverted spring.

Rania was nervous that day. She closed herself in her room and refused to see anybody. She was facing the sea. It was restless. For three days it had stormed. It would not yet recognize the sun and its cerulean realm. It angered at the coast. The gigantic depths were heaving still. Was not peace a folly; light, a mockery to beguile the earth to tear sap from her lusty flesh, to play with fruit and seeds; then what? The brown terrified death of rainless summer that would lay bare the earth, were it not for the fog-mercy.

A helpless sadness weighed upon her; the deluding power of life was unbearable. Why the endless, unappeasable thirst for the together state? Why this gripping, gnawing lust of eyes and mind and soul, of ears and stomach to be fed with some other substance, to be drunk with potent glamor which leaves only bitterness and questions never answered, never to be solved—yet luring on, luring on, dissonances stretched into excruciating tenuity toward impossible resolutions? What a wearisome farce this play of change, from self to not-self, from one to many, and many to oneness, and then silence, nonbeing, dreaming. Why not dreaming a little deeper, beyond recall? Weariness, infinite weariness Oh, for one that would lull away into senseless sleep, into endless atony! Where can that be? Through what beyond, into what silence . . . more pain needed perhaps; more pounding, crushing, corroding? And then; and then? . . . Her mind reeled into blankness. It slipped away, a soft thing of the sea, swayed by vast tides of unconscious dream. It slipped away where names no longer lie with boundaries, and the smiles of things no longer betray the changeless No-thing.

She did not hear the door open; light invade the darkened room. She did not move as Mrs. Falkner called, hastened to her, kneeled beside her and shook her head drooped as a broken wing. She did not see Hilda hurrying for cold water, salts; then a tall figure enter, slowly; deep grey eyes peer through her. Overbearing silence; what rite of destiny was being consummated? The dark head came near hers, long Oriental hands touched her eyes, pressed again the revulsed orbit. No; it was not time yet to dream deep beyond recall. It must be that the other was telling some awesome name that had power to bring back, from beyond boundaries; mysterious name heavy with the meaning of destiny, heavy with the silence and depth of destiny—heavy name that strikes the swaying soul and overturns her flight, turns it back toward the earth, where men crawl in passion of godhood beneath the sneers of sea gulls and eagles.

—◦◦◇◦◦—

When she opened at last her consciousness to the light, the deep grey eyes shone first into her renewed world; two deep wells of silence and immateriality filled with loneliness that was peace, compassion that was tender yet firm. She shook her head gently and smiled: "Why did you call me back? What more can I do? I am so tired."

The grey eyes glowed a little; they clouded. A strange sullenness gripped the contracting pupils. "We are all tired, my friend, but we must all go on, just the same . . . just the same."

She nodded. She was willing. She would take up her post at the great wall of protection, shielding baby-men, enwombing the prenatal milleniums of the new manhood—long, long milleniums of darkness and gestation.

When she looked around she saw kind faces surrounding her. Mrs. Falkner, Hilda, the young Robert Johnson who loved her, the sturdy Russian face of Peter Harbin in whose silences icebergs floated in long silvery files, the closed yet mellow oval of Sylvia Rutherford who dared not forget all the tortured knowledge gleaned in English "occult" circles . . . a few others that stood near the door. Rania turned her head slowly, closing in their burdens, weighing. She smiled—a little painful smile, accepting, welcoming. Boris was still watching her intently. She stared at him. She flung herself at him in the passion of an eye gesture that tore through the space between them and sank into him like a firebolt hitting metal. His eyes closed. It was accomplished. Destinies were knotted once again; a mysterious unearthly knot that was to hold together many sundered souls, world-scattered, helpless, in widowhood of God.

Boris stood up, glanced at Mrs. Falkner who said a few cheering words and brought the company downstairs. Hilda, her face pale and frozen by something she could not fully grasp, yet which blew upon her as a snow-heavied wind, helped Rania to follow. Near the fireplace, where roots of manzanita were burning with white fervent light, Boris stood: a lean tree of silence whose head seemed more a root from above than an earth-growing top, with the strange will-strength of a root often found in true occultists' faces, a strength which is not meant to be seen, as a root is not meant to be seen.

Then he spoke, calmly, fluently, with the singing yet guttural voice of the Slavs. He spoke about the inner ruler, the God within. With strong forceful words he bared the shams of the so-called religious life in which sinning man prays to a far-off God for intercession and redemption. He sang the hidden powers that reside in man's own heart, the fire that can make him god if controlled by knowledge and character, or devil if dammed in for self-gratification. He showed that the path to power and divinity can only originate in self-denial, intelligent compassion and enlightened service. To his hearers he portrayed the conditions of the Iron Age in which we are living; he expounded the duty incumbent on those who are willing to work in utter consecration to the task of upholding the great universal seed-truths of Man, even while nearly all humanity is rushing on the road to disintegration and chemical reabsorption into unselved matter. His voice rang, a call for servers and trustees, for noble and strong characters who would join the company of the few great souls who stand and unfalteringly remain witnesses to truth and spiritual harmony—watchers, guides, admonishers, masters of life.

A profound pause followed his words, as if space had been filled with such overwhelming substance of life that minds were breathing heavily to reestablish the balance of their slower rhythms. Rania had closed her eyes. Her mouth had contracted a little, as if to repress tears. In the silence of all these human souls trying to regain their disconnected unity of being and to capture two or three ideas which had found access into their mind's womb and would perhaps grow into living realities, Rania sensed, almost saw, some majestic presence. She looked at Boris, composed and vaguely smiling in keen yet gracious expectancy. The same smooth root-strength of mystery. A sense of effortless tension; as if a heavy parturition had taken place through him, yet it did not exactly affect him; only the nerves somewhat shook, as lead pipes through which steam is forced.

Then conversation broke in, animated and cordial. Small groups started real debates. A few little "I"s began to swell considerably in the process. Mrs. Falkner brought in hot chocolate and fruit tarts. Hilda and other girls helped to pass the cups. Boris talked to this or that group, laughing off silly questions, throwing vital hints into this or that eager and restless mind. He did not come near Rania, who kept quiet and disappeared soon after he had ceased talking, pretending fatigue. As she reached the stairs, she turned back. He was fixing strongly his gaze upon her, over the shoulders of a couple of men with whom he was apparently chattering. She smiled and bowed her head.

Step after step she climbed, leaning on her crutches, a hollowed life, with sorrow-broken limbs, shattered body–going on, through, going on . . . with deep vacant eyes open to infinitudes where nevertheless there was a name for her to answer to, a post to hold, a destiny to fulfill.

And she went on toward that destiny.

—∞◇∞—

CHAPTER III

She lay awake until the noises of departing guests, of shutting doors, the many customary sounds that prelude the repose of human beings, were engulfed one by one in the silence, and there was left but the heavy rhythmical breathing of that silence out of the sea. Thoughts began then to ebb and flow in her mind like tides confused by emerging rocks breaking the quiet surge of the moon-drawn waters. A huge pointing mass stood, parting these brain-tides; a light-tower, it seemed, pointing to a way – which way?

She knew it in her soul to be Boris. He had emerged from the sullen depth of destiny and confronted the ship that had lost harbor and drifted round its North Star, a star so far above that it failed to point to any horizontal course, showing only vertical unearthly immensities. He had emerged, a rock bearing an earth-focused flame. Though the ray of light did not yet pierce the darkness with the certitude of a goal, at least it threw upon the limitless expanse of life a path. A path draws to its treading the exile. It calls one to its presumable end, to the lure of a somewhere

---

that would give meaning to the path. Or is it that the path itself is its own meaning and justification?

The path drew, had power. She could feel the little molecules of her soul trembling like iron filings subjected to a magnet; they quiver, they rebel, they rush upon each other in sudden tragic excitement; they are torn in confusion from their natural agglomerated state; they stammer silently bewildered questions; they lift themselves, point upward, tragic unfinished ends. And the quivering subsides—quickly for us, but how slowly for the vertiginous atoms! There has come direction. The metal dust has taken form, meaning. It tells the tale of cosmic energy that radiates through them, that orders them, that gives them significance.

Rania felt herself being ordered into a new meaning, into the meaning perhaps which was the flower toward which her life-stalk had grown painfully, stubbornly, beyond her conscious will. It hurt. Something was crying inside, was being torn; some dear, sweet voice was bewailing a consummation, which nevertheless it knew unavoidable. It only wanted to be heard a little longer, a little longer to sing its lovesong, its beautiful earth-born tones which had lost bitterness and understood, yet were brokenhearted, poor flapping wings of pain.

Late in the night she fell asleep. But consciousness went on in a strange forbidding way. The shapes and lights she had often dreamt of during her youth appeared again. But now they seemed no longer to be outside, but within her. She herself was shapes and lights churned by an unseen, yet felt presence for some mysterious alchemy. She was it, yet not entirely it. A strange feeling of duality pervaded her inner being. She was no longer an eye, but more like a vast ear vibrating to sound-shapes that struck its quivering strings. These sounds were outside, yet she was them. She was the utterer and the recipient. She told herself words she could not yet understand.

Something then seemed to happen, as if an awesome decision had been made final, irrevocable. Something trembled frantically within. It seemed the whole world was shaking with a vision of expectancy. And presently a huge fiery mass triangularly shaped at the lower end, cubical above, was seen, which was lowered into her very soul and being. It seared. It hollowed the soft soul-substance, as a hot iron the flesh. The agony of it was horrible, almost unbearable. Tears streamed from the sleeping face. Rania awoke, shattered by uncontrollable sobs. She bit her lips, choked her moaning with the sheets. Pain, excruciating pain   pain which seemed to have no cause, which racked the soul.

When she regained somewhat her peace, she remembered vaguely symbolical dreams, the meaning of which at one moment seemed illuminating, at others to vanish into sheer fancy. Some majestic figure had put a white and gold mantle upon her; it was so heavy. She could hardly bear it; as she was near collapsing, the walls opened and there was a heap of little children calling, hand-stretching toward her, famished . . . and wolves sprang from the dark and bled them to death, crushed their bones. Then a great storm arose within a sea which was made of houses and trees and fields. A steamer was sinking amidst heavy fumes, fog perhaps or smoke. . . She was hurrying, grabbing a man or two. Then the jump; far off land barely visible through the black darkness . . . a voice in the distance calling . . . she caught only a word or two . . . "sacrifice . . . willing victim. . . " Then it was the room again. She tried to take away the white mantle. It became a shroud. It clung to the flesh. Someone tore it. Inside, it was red with her own blood. She was alone, naked. Men passed by who stared at her, who sneered, spit at her. Then her body became changed into the likeness of pulsating triangles, cubes, cylinders. Wheels whirled, huge sledgehammers pounded flesh into form. A great wind rose with swirling dust. Dust became earth; it clung to her. She became a stone of strangely shaped mass. Mortar was being poured from above. She saw there were other stone-masses like her; they were all being cemented together. They stood like a wall. Icy gales pounded upon the outer surface. The wall contracted with a strange rhythm like living tissue. She had become a little cell in the skin of some immense being. At times, poisonous acrid matter passed through, coming from within, released through her. In the within, she felt lives dreaming beautiful deeds, eager young minds playing and loving . . . happy.

—∞◇∞—

She did not plunge again into the whirlpool of dreams. She stared with wide opened eyes into the dawn, bubbling in ripples of effervescent silver from behind the pines. She tried to remember the motion picture of images and scenes which had barely reached her through the befogged rough lens of her brain. If she closed her eyes, the dreams might fall again behind the counter of memory, lost in dust and chaos. She summoned them tensely, trying to pin them against the brightening window so that she might inspect them and give them meaning. But the very effort caused the evanescent phantasms to slip away, as unnoticed hours of happiness slip away leaving emptiness in their trail. She rose, as the sun—afraid of the immensity of the sky—was gathering scarves of fog to narrow down the blue steppes; or was it compassion for men that caused him to veil his too glorious face from their littleness? Men have died from seeing the face of destiny . . . but Rania would not die. It would be too easy to fade away and cease to remember one's name. The name must be uttered, in purity, in solemn strength. She felt the silence thunder it forth. That was the awesome, inescapable event, the seed of all the fantastic night-dreams. She had heard the name of her destiny. She had been utterer and recipient. Within her being, all was connected now. *That* she could remember, even if the name itself seemed lost. Not lost though . . . each year, or cycle of years, would sound out one of its letters. Living had to reveal to consciousness the fullness of the mystery which dreams only reflect, a moonlike unsteady glow of remembrance.

As she opened her door to go downstairs, Hilda was standing with strange troubled eyes, imploring, feverish. Why was she up so early? Rania asked. Was she not well? Hilda shrugged her shoulders. No, she did not sleep. She could not sleep. She could not stop thoughts coming and going, aimless mob. Rania looked at her intently. There was something tense and tragic in the girl. She had the over-focused, yet unsteady, look of uncontrollable passion, or fanaticism. It had become more and more accentuated during the last weeks; but this morning—was it lack of sleep?—it glowed ominously. She struggled to veil it with a smile, a joke; but she stammered, and Boris's name jumped out of her throat, a wild horse spurred by a passionate rider. So, there was the strain center. Boris! Boris! . . . How did Rania like him? His voice? He certainly did not soften his answers to foolish questions. . . Boris! Boris!

Rania answered little. She was facing Hilda intently. She was trying to sink herself into the soul shattered by feverish emotional waves. She had to know. She had to feel the hurt; perhaps she could soothe it, or guide it toward creative transmutations. She tried not to think, but to vibrate up and down the scale until she would hit the spot of resonance, where she would be tuned to Hilda's magnetic storm and, absorbing such resonance, could realize the full meaning and the source of the upheaval.

They prepared coffee on the electric stove, toast. Hilda felt chilly. These awful fogs, would they never stop? The sun was all obscured now. Was the face of destiny too strong? Too strong releases of power shatter the weak steel. The blood of men is not well tempered. Its iron turns too red, too fiercely hot; or it stiffens in cold rigidity making the life brittle. Nervousness . . . and some deep pulling wound. The heart contracts. The universe seen through it takes distorted shapes, an unfocused lens image. Suddenly a great pain and lassitude invaded Rania. Hilda had left to get wood for the fire. The room felt dreadfully empty. All the things in it hurt in angular resentment. There was too much power everywhere. The things could not stand it. Hilda could not stand it. Must little destinies be jolted out of harmony, where great destinies flare into combustion? Must the fire scorch their thin covering, baring them to the winds of astral destruction? The tragedy of it!

Rania felt like laughing, bitterly, sneeringly. Such a pitiless, brutal life! Such a comedy, too! For one moment she hated Boris, hated herself. Such foolishness to talk big words, spirituality, progress, compassion! The simplest thing of life meant always more or less death to someone. One could not move, breathe, feel, love without destroying some harmony, murdering some forms of joy, contentment, some poor human dream of beauty! And to what end? God, to what end? . . . if only the end were clear. But no, mirages always, dreams, hallucinations, which the mind takes hold of, as building stones! Hallucinations, hallucinations all. She laughed. The laugh rang so hoarse, so sinister that Hilda, who had just crossed the doorstep, became frightened, let the logs drop. One fell upon her foot. She screamed with pain, yet ran to Rania, trembling, weeping. "What is it, Rania?"

In a flash Rania saw the whole situation; she felt the hurt toes; the girl's body quivered in her own; the strained mind, the long repressed fermenting emotions were hitting against her own heart. It was pitiful, tragic, useless. What to do? What to do? She took Hilda in her arms, smiled on her as on a baby at the breast who beats with little raving fists. She forced her to take off her shoe. She poured cold water, some soothing unguent. She felt Hilda tremble as she held her leg firmly, bandaging the foot. She looked at her eyes; they were distant, tense, almost revulsed.

Boris came again for dinner. Yes, he had had a very fine day, mostly of rest. He had been touring so much, lecturing through so many states, always going, talking, shaking hands, receiving confessions, answering questions, pouring himself, resisting the suction of unsteady minds and emotional womanhood, yet not resisting, being open, flowing outward. It felt good now, such cool pine-rest and the effulgent white sand on which he had lain for hours in the half-sun in a glow of ultraviolet light reverberated from sand to mist.

Mrs. Falkner guiltily enumerated for him several invitations for lunch, teas, picnics which the phone had brought during the day. He laughed. Of course rest was always meant as a relative figure of speech. He would accept all, do what he could. Soon he was perhaps to begin the writing of some long books which he had in mind for a year or two, but had had no time to concentrate upon. Perhaps Carmel would be the place—he glanced at Rania, who avoided him. Perhaps conditions would be favorable. He had felt already the tremendous power of the coast, of rocks and trees and winds. He had sensed things of the past. There must be a meaning in it all. If we knew the history of old continents, of immensely old civilizations, we would know fully.

He told about the universal traditions corroborated by modern geologists concerning the old Pacific or Lemurian continent. He had found many references to it while in India, in Java and other islands. It had been said that a few portions of the California coast had been parts of that continent, its eastern coast then. Obviously to him Carmel and the surroundings must be one of such remnants of the most archaic land, disappeared perhaps millions of years ago. When such fragments of lands remain, it is because they were especially important magnetic centers of the old continent. Perhaps great cities, or temples, or occult retreats had been built there. Though these be destroyed now, the very soil is still penetrated by the very powers of old, revitalized under the sway of some recurring cycle.

Mrs. Falkner questioned, interrupted him. Her acquaintance with Eastern and occult literature made it easy for her to enter into the spirit of such ideas. Her mind was active and reliable. She had deliberately drawn a veil upon her past. Now she lived for the joy of knowledge, the stimulation of great books into which flowed all her love-nature. She knew perhaps that the magic circle she had thus drawn around herself was somewhat of a shell, but she was always eager to look outward from it through well-devised windows, which besides would bring more light into the room of her loving.

Boris Khsantianoff was to her such a window. She had felt at once as she met him that here was a man in whom knowledge was alive and real; a man who did not look at men from the pages of worshiped books or the summit of some remote mountain, but who was passing through an intense and, she sensed, rather tumultuous life extracting universal meanings, sending forth a straight message of noble living and continuing in some way some old chain of influence, now rousing a new vitality, a new courage in those who were ready to listen. Intellectually, she was curious to know how he had reached that point, to know his teachers, the influences which made him what he was. Intellectually. At the bottom of her heart she was slightly jealous and slightly afraid he might be a little upsetting to her tranquillity and her peaceful studies.

spiritual flowering

She would not admit, of course, that she was jealous or envious. Yet there was in her this queer biting feeling that he was a living exponent of truths of which she only knew the wording in books. She was conscious enough of her own little selfishness in being comfortable to resent subtly the fact that he did not seem to care about any moral and mental comfort, but was living a hazardous, dangerous, self-denying life. She knew she dared not live such a life. She felt condemned in herself by herself, because of the mere fact of his being what he was. Her personal pride was hurt; even though she was profoundly devoted to the ideals Boris expounded and sincerely admired his work and his nature.

Hilda was silent. At times she stared at Boris almost violently, as if she wanted to tear his being open and do something to him, anything—love him, hate him, destroy him, kiss him, but something to make him feel that she was there, that he had to take account of her, had to be disturbed, and be different from himself, be something that she would have made him be. Then she would glance at Rania who looked at Boris with wide eyes, drawn in, very quiet, very silent—yet avoiding him, as if hurt, the moment he would turn to her. And in Hilda's look there crept a strange hollow light, light of blinded eyes, light which could see no more light, but only dream it from remembrance . . . something burnt out, sad and desperate, made almost cruel by the twisting of the mouth that told tales of repressed pain and bitter suppression.

And so the evening passed. An early departure, after a couple of friends had called and greeted Khsantianoff. Human beings drawn in together within manmade walls, symbols perhaps of·greater enclosements of destiny; human beings struggling, caught in a slow chemistry of emotions, of yearnings, of dissatisfactions, of whirring minds—test tubes for combinations of tense and fervent wills.

Time grinds, pulverizes. Time, and the heat of soul and body energy aroused by proximity and contacts, work steadily, pushing the operation to its mysterious conclusion. The great chemist whose mind has mastered the molecular laws of life may have calculated wisely the ultimate reactions. But beyond these laws there lies the realm of man the free. Free not to alter the unavoidable events, but to give them the meaning he wills, the meaning he *is*. Free to use the explosive energy of power generating, fateful and cyclic commixtures, for the all or for the self. For if power is of nature, the use of power is of man. In that lies man's destiny.

The night was clear, speared by stars. The moon was haloing tall pines. It threw shadows on the dirt roads of Carmel, scarred by rains, pelted with cracking needles. Boris passed by his little cottage at the end of San Antonio and walked toward the sands. They shone like phosphorescent substance. They were cold to the feet. They were soft and sinuous, giving in to the stamping of the man's walk. Tomorrow though, the wind would blow and what would remain of the manmade hollows? What does ever remain?... Boris felt disturbed and saddened. He sensed the weight of the inescapable on his life, the pressure of destiny upon his heart.

"Stop," said the firm hand, "and listen. Death balances life, action, reaction. Souls have converged, to be equated into new and vaster destiny. Past and future. The present fluctuates. It wants meaning to become eternal." What meaning?

Boris walks along the shore. Huge breakers curve and fall. They hit violently the sands. In their wake, the sands are smooth and pure, virginal, remade into the likeness of infinite space. Life is a pounding sea upon the molecules of soul. Each molecule is a past, the shell or seed of lives we were. One after the other they have been drawn ashore above the sea, above life into consciousness. On these soul-shores, sun and moon beat, and events stamp their steps. But the tides surge with cyclic grandeur, with waves of destiny making men whole anew; the marks of events, makers of impermanent selfhood, are washed away. Who among men know themselves as shores, rather than as little hollows ploughed by events and softened by winds? Who among men are welcoming the sea, destroyer of hollows and of names? Who among men know themselves as the sea, maker of shores, womb of lives, sands of tomorrow?

Boris sinks himself into a dream, into a soul. She surges with the sea; she is the sea; she hammers at the shore of his selfhood; she is torn against rocks, against the compact mob of prenatal humanity. Beautiful strong singing soul! He sees the lineaments of a glorious form of self, in which is power and endurance, compassion for the age. He watches it shrink into a broken frame, which men call Rania. It faces him. It is an interrogation, a probing, a sounding. How deep is he, Boris Khsantianoff, whom men applaud, respect, and women yearn for for self-deliverance and motherhood? How deep and pure, the pool that reflects light and gives comfort to thirsting ones? It is easy to be pure where nature sways in rhythms of bounty and innocence. But the cities—these dark, bleak, morbid brothels of wanderers and lost souls! To go through, to dwell in them, to accept them, yet be pure, yet be true to the glorious forms of that other world and dance the fateful deeds of existence with craving souls that fasten upon you with greedy eyes and wound you with their despair, their sucking emptiness and meaningless-ness—how difficult, how excruciating!

For four years now he had traveled through America bringing the message his life had grown, like a fruit, during a period of awesome struggle. The weight of these four years seemed almost unbeara-ble. Oh, what longing for repose does come to one in whom has blown for weary months the chill of commercial cities and frozen egos! Repose, repose of which he had seen glorious relics in Asiatic lands . . . repose at the breast of dreams wherein sings the fullness and untouched splendor of self . . . repose, perhaps, within the tenderness of beloved eyes and kind hands that weave a cloak of silence and peace round the bruised soul, the parched consciousness. Men are such fools when they dream of love! Like children whose limbs crave gestures, they distort "being" into "making" love, into fallacious motions in which there is no soul.

Boris wandered back in front of Rania's home. All was silent, dark windows. Could he not pierce through the walls, pierce through the flesh-covers of these three beings and behold their true stations, and their self-made fates to which he knew himself bound—for what consummation? Perhaps he could. He had been taught releases of consciousness which might bare to him the inner beings of the sleeping ones. But no, it could not be done; it ought not to be done. This body was the field to work out destiny—for him. Some day perhaps the other doors would fully and legitimately open. Today the duty was here, the test was here. He would face it in stoic calm, in complete sincerity and openness.

That night Rania saw in dream a great white-clad figure approach her as she was bending over the earth near a tree. It was glowing with fire and seemed to carry with it the hot breath of deserts. Behind it, as in a mirage, she could discern oases, lakes with strange structures, tall men with majestic mien. The mirage seemed to be like one of these images formed in the air by experimental lenses. The white figure was the lens; somehow she was the inverted reflection. It was not clear. But there was in her a sense of elation, of having become many, of having absorbed many, of being the image of some great concourse—narrowed down, blurred, still a true image. Between image and reality stood the tall man who, she felt, was Boris, though there was so much light radiating from the face that she could see no definite features. He began to intone curious words that sounded as from some other world, sounds that grew into shapes and lights crowded with the onrush of elemental force that sought entrance into her. She hesitated a moment, then tore her own clothes that hung heavily. And suddenly she began to glow. The outlines of her body lost themselves in waves of radiance. Streams of fire sprang up from her loins. They tore through her body, struck her head that ached with excruciating pain. She cried:

"I am going blind! I cannot! I cannot!"

The light and images disappeared; only two deep grey eyes, full of sadness and silence were fixed upon her. They slowly became dim and closed.

—∞◇∞—

The following day she told Mrs. Falkner she wanted to speak to Boris alone. She would walk to his house across the road. Mrs. Falkner looked at her, inquiringly, then said:

"All right! I am sure he will be glad to talk to you. He said nice things about you."

"What did he say?" Rania exclaimed.

"I have forgotten the words. He inquired about your accident. We told him how brave you had been and he seemed deeply moved and sympathetic."

Rania bowed her head, smiled a little and slowly moved across the road, her body weighing upon the crutches.

She stopped at the cottage's entrance. A small wooden gate was covered with wild roses, untrimmed. Tall lupins were crowding around the rustic walls. She could hear the wood crackling in the fireplace through the half-opened window. Boris was walking up and down the studio-room slowly, meditatively, with bent shoulders, closed eyes. He must have felt some presence, as he suddenly turned around and glanced through the window. She walked on and met him as he opened the door. A strange joyous look shone in his face.

"Welcome! It is lovely of you to come. Did you walk alone?"

Certainly, she was feeling strong these days. She craved exercise. Perhaps some day she might be well enough to walk without the awful wooden sticks. He inquired intently upon the condition of her legs. Was there any hope that she might dispense with her crutches? She really did not know. Her doctor thought in a year or so another operation might be attempted. She was trying to get strong, then would go to Chicago or New York to consult surgeons who were known to have accomplished remarkable cures.

For a while they were silent. She was staring at the moving fire. It reminded her of her dream. It became very vivid, sharp. She could almost feel again the scorching of the up-reaching flame that shattered her. Boris was sitting, leaning against a table, his hands somewhat nervously playing with papers. Then without lifting her glance from the burning wood, she said in slow almost inaudible tones:

"There has been fire, too, in my body that has burned me. It has torn through me. It has brought me pain, much pain. People call it fever, call it love, call it . . . I do not know what. But I know it is fire. It has come again." Her voice rose a little. "It has come again, because of you. And you know it." She turned facing him.

A little startled, his eyes widened.

"You have brought me fire once more, but another fire. There is nothing more to break in my body; so it burns my soul now, it burns my dreams; it burns all of me, Boris. And you know it! You know it! Don't you?"

Yes, he knew. He had felt there must come some arousal out of their meeting. When he had first seen her in her faint, almost gone, he had realized at once that they were both parts of one single reality, group, brotherhood . . . names mattered little. He had watched her. He had felt the rich pulse of her life. Perhaps they had a mission together, a duty to fulfill.

"I know you, Rania. I know you are strong and brave. I know you have suffered much and loved much. I can read many lines of your face, and perhaps the halo of your whole being. But what I cannot read, because I would not want to even if I could, is: what does it mean to you that I have come, that you have entered this room? There are meanings that are rich with power and truth; others that destroy. What new meaning can you give to that fire which you say is now burning you?"

Rania looked straight in his eyes. Something poignant was tearing through her. It swelled into the space between them. It made it heavy, tense; it made minutes stagger, insensible of duration. Her voice answered almost automatic, white, toneless: "My meaning shall be your meaning."

His mouth contracted; a smile perhaps, perhaps pain. He arose. He stood straight against the fire. His face became very grave, very solemn. It trembled a little as he answered: "May our meaning be true, Rania!"

For a long while she kept her head bowed as under the weight of a visitation; then she lifted it up, a little shaking, an open question raised to the sun of an accepted certainty, which nevertheless had not yet penetrated the entire consciousness. "How can we know the truth and be sure?"

Boris smiled. He took in his hands her fingers that trembled. "The truth is that which we are able to experience fully, creatively. There is no absolute truth, but every moment has its own sanctuary in which life celebrates its mystery, which is the endless birth of truth."

The silence became solemn as if growing out of some mystical ceremony in which presences were communing. A voice murmured words which tongues hardly uttered, words which seeped through heart chambers into this world of strange conflagrations.

"I dedicate my life to the highest truth that is my destiny. I consecrate my life to the service of all. I am my destiny. I am my truth. May we both become the fullness of this truth which calls us to union, in freedom and joy! May we fulfill together our greatest destiny!"

Rania bowed her head caressed by the dancing phantasmagoria of the fire. Strong, rugged logs were melting in the embrace of the greater reality; and this embrace was radiance. Boris pressed her hands, which had known how to accept destiny in the fullness of moments intensely lived. The race in her had been broken; her body, splintered, maimed by the pressure of a passion whose roots were deep into long ancestral pasts. But the invisible race also called, toward the future, to equate the past with this future. A dedication had appeared, had struck the resonant substance of this moment, rich beyond all earthly passion. She saw its outlines glowing in the burning logs, in Boris's deep eyes lighted by other flames, intangible and pure. Yes, she would offer her life to its greatest destiny. Words rose from her lips, words majestic with acceptance, with serenity and vision.

Silence fell beyond the words. Where there is little separateness left, words suffice to break the walls, to cause the commixture of the life fluids of the souls. On their quivering trail the peace of completion sweeps like a great wing of stars. It infinitizes two souls into wholeness.

—∞◇∞—

CHAPTER IV

When Rania announced at the dinner table that she was going to study every day with Boris's help certain phases of Oriental philosophy, a startled look appeared on Mrs. Falkner's face, while Hilda became very pale and hollow, as if something had dropped within her and her life was ebbing away uncontained. Boris, who was gazing intently on her, frowned and some sudden sadness seemed to steal over his features. But he shook it off at once and rejoined, saying that he had himself urged Rania to study more seriously than she had done before, and that knowing the difficulty of such an abstract study he had offered to act as a guide. As he knew Sanskrit fairly well, he could thus supplement the translations, or point out the root-meaning of terms and names used so often in occult literature. He added he would be very happy besides to conduct a class on similar subjects if a few persons were ready to devote themselves wholeheartedly to the work.

Mrs. Falkner, with a voice not too assured, said something to Rania about her having to be thankful for such a teacher to help her. It was so difficult often to find one's way alone. Boris tried to turn the conversation to a happier mood by joking about himself. He laughed at the term "teacher." Not as much however as at being called "Dr." Khsantianoff. Rania joined him in amusement. Yes, that certainly sounded funny. Dr. Khsantianoff! Hilda could not refrain from saying, half sarcastically:

"Of course, Boris sounds much better!"

A strange bitterness gripped her. Boris tried to analyze it, to discover the deeper roots of the feeling. There was something in her that somewhat antagonized him. Had he allowed such an impulsive reaction to become visible to Hilda? He tried to be more kind than before to her. She was suffering. He had pity for her. He asked her many questions about hospital work and her experiences. But she did not relax; she seemed able to speak only of Rania's sickness, and Rania's courage, and Rania's pains. She seemed to take pleasure in enumerating all the bones Rania had had broken, all the terrible things that had happened to her.

Rania had taken paper and pencil and was drawing Boris's face. He had to be quiet and not to move his head. Mrs. Falkner was sewing. The atmosphere was tense, uneasy. After an hour the drawing was finished. It told in bold lines, in accentuated masses and sharp outlines, a poem of strength and tragic fervor. Hilda exclaimed:

"She certainly did not make you look happy! Much older too. She always does that. She drew me and I looked like a ghost."

But Boris was gazing deeply on the drawing. It seemed to open to him and he was finding in it a depth of himself which was not so familiar, but which he felt very intensely true, implacably true. Mrs. Falkner remarked that a man of his spirituality should radiate a much greater peace; that he did radiate such; but the drawing was almost tortured. Rania seemed to invest everything, rocks, trees, men, with her own tragedy.

Rania smiled at first, looking at Boris and attempting to feel his deepest emotion in front of her vision of him; but at the last remark she retorted rather sharply that contentment was easy for oysters and cows. Hilda laughed. "Hurrah for the oysters!" she shouted, bitingly.

Rania was confused. Why make fun of such a plain statement? Was not humanity today in a most tragic period of her growth? Tragedy did not mean bitterness or despair. It meant confrontation. Why hide the torments of men and bejewel them with false happiness? Why make faces look like dolls, without any lines, without any of the furrows that the pageant of moments plough into the flesh? Was she not right? She asked Boris with almost passionate pleading.

Yes, she was right, as far as he could see. He did not find much value in American optimism; it was lovely, but childlike. It was really a false mental attitude, a deep refusal to face reality, a mode of escape. Escape! That was the great curse, the source of all evil. Religions are all born out of the craving to escape; drugs are modes of escape. Alas! much of so-called intellectual studies, much even of love—sentimental, indrawing love—are but subtler forms of escape.

Perhaps it was his Slav ancestry, perhaps all the horrors he had seen in Russia, in Asia, everywhere; perhaps it was that he had not yet the strength of becoming, beyond it all, at peace. Still, he was at peace. Because within himself he accepted it whole and understood, his inner self was not affected. That alone was the refuge; but a refuge in the midst of the battle, a refuge of understanding in the thick of strong, fervent action, in the thick of war. Could the warrior look polished like a bishop, and ethereal like a cave ascetic?

spiritual flowering

Could one who knew the world misery and had vowed to serve the cause of the future against the past, the cause of spiritual freedom, could he live unbruised, unseared, unbleeding in his outer self?

Rania had felt in him the warrior-self; probably because she herself was of the same race of warrior-selves. She had told in lines of struggle the fury of the battle that had raged, that was raging still, always would rage until the new Golden Age would lift man up from his own hells and make darkness significant in terms of light. Darkness and light are twins. Could one draw a picture without the black ink? Could there be form, movement, rhythm without the contrast of lights and shadows? Chiaroscuro was not only a technique valuable to painters: it was a technique of living, a great occult mystery. If only men understood the mysteries of the alchemical generation of power! Is Adeptship possible where there is no power? Power means rupture of equilibrium, terrific tensions induced, maintained and controlled between the most widely separated extremes. The identification of the opposites . . . the ultimate secret of mastery!

Boris stopped suddenly. Rania had closed her eyes, very near him. He felt her breath, rhythmical, moving through him. But he dared not look at her. Hilda was staring at them both, like a wounded beast caught in a hunter's trap. Mrs. Falkner was trying very hard to remember by heart all that the great man said, to serve it to friends as occasions would arise. It fitted well the carefully dusted compartments in her brains. It was quite exciting. It was her form of escape. She drank wisdom like champagne. It made her feel good.

Boris stopped. His voice had sounded suddenly like a bitter joke to him. He felt the need of all his sense of humor not to sink in utter depression. He must leave. He could not stand the friction of these fates grinding his own being in curiosity, in hatred, even in love.

He felt a yearning to be alone; never to speak any longer. For it is strange how one's soul flees at the very tips of uttered words, its radiation lost in the void of uncomprehending and disturbed minds—uselessly lost or contaminated.

As if she had understood, Rania, gently but with a strange firmness, put her hand upon his shoulder and said: "You would like hot chocolate, wouldn't you, before going? It is chilly outdoors. I think it will rain tomorrow. I am aching in all my bones . . . a marvelous barometer I am now."

Somehow the tension had been broken. He thanked her. Yes, hot chocolate; an excellent idea. Hilda, with nervous haste, rushed to the kitchen without saying a word; and in a few moments brought back the steaming cups.

Just then the phone rang from Monterey. A telegram from the south for Mr. Khsantianoff. Would he not come for a series of lectures in Los Angeles? A group was formed and expected him within two or three weeks, if possible. Boris hesitated a while, looked at Rania. He read the message aloud. Hilda burst out excitedly: "Will you go?"

He smiled, a little sadly. "I suppose I shall go. I have to go where I am called."

"But you will be back, will you not?" inquired Mrs. Falkner.

"Probably."

The clock struck amidst the silence. Boris asked permission to leave. Rania pressed his hand as he bid her good night. He thought there were tears pressing around her eyes. He smiled tenderly.

spiritual flowering

"May I keep my portrait? I would love to show it to friends in the south."

She assented, then words had to leave her lips that had contracted: "But you must promise to pose for another, a better one?"

"I promise."

—∞◇∞—

The next day Rania walked to Boris's house. The door was unlatched and on a paper tablet hanging in Carmel fashion from a nail alongside the door was written "Shall be back soon." She hesitated for a moment; it was damp, almost raining. She went inside. The fireplace was still warm. She twisted and lighted some newspapers, built a small hollow cone of pine wood. The flame flared up, resinous. She sat in front of it, warming her aching limbs that felt the rain. She glanced around. She felt the silence, almost weighing it like gold in the hollow of a hand. It was rich and enfolding. One could sense peace caressing all the little things, like a scarf scented with living skin. The peace lived. Rania let herself go. She stretched her soul into it, as a swimmer, cold-bitten, who encounters a warm current and relaxes, floating on the soft eiderdown waves.

Oh, to feel always such a pure tranquillity around one's being, to merge into its silence and its fullness, and be harmonized, be happy! Only for a few moments while living with her old friend in the Hollywood canyon had she tasted something that felt like happiness. But here there was more. There was intensity, subdued fervor, a richness of humanhood that spelt overcoming, triumph, heroism; not merely the serenity of one who has quieted into being wise and old.

Soon Boris came. He seemed to bring everything to a focus. Around him the silence took meaning. It ran to him to be blessed, to be given significance and human warmth. And her entire being within the broken frame followed the silence. It yearned for significance, to be made whole, to be opened.

It said: "Take me. I have waited for you. I am rich of substance. I am fruitful. Take me, beloved! What am I if untaken? What am I without the name you shall give me? I am folding around you to receive the whole. I am being you all around you. Take me. Make me whole."

He stood silent, holding her two hands that had flown to him to be captured. He looked far away, far away through her. She was all open, a great door of life. His self flowed through, not hurting, not bruising. There can be no hurt where there are no walls hemming in love. He pulsated through her whole being as a center through a sphere, a rhythm of the true love beyond limits, beyond the narrow channel of the coercive and coherent flesh, beyond the spelling of names. He was seeing through her, as mind through eyes. She was eye; he was vision; and beyond both the one Self saw, the Perceiver, the Spectator, the Enjoyer.

Soon the silence became so full of wholeness that brains and body could stand the weight of it no longer.

She said: "Are you really going?"

"I must, Rania."

"But you shall come back soon, stay here then—or else? . . . or else, could I not go, too?"

He smiled. "And then? What should we do then?" he asked.

spiritual flowering

She did not answer. She was feeling her path through something dark and huge she could not well fathom. She looked up to him again, jokingly:

"Then we shall study of course!"

He laughed. "Why not now?"

He drew near them a little table crowded with books; and they began to read.

—∞◇∞—

Two weeks more before going. She came almost every day for a couple of hours and they studied in intense rich concentration. He went from book to book, culling here and there sentences, paragraphs pregnant with meaning. New horizons burst open before her, like flower buds in tropical springs. The topography of a world in which she had dwelt only as a blind man became clear, evident. She could see reliefs, mountains, plains, where before she had roamed through poignant fogs, in feeling, not in knowledge. As the fog lifted she recognized the landscapes. She knew all the time they were there; but she had forgotten shapes and names. Now it all came back with terrific power. Her heart would beat violently as she would read a sentence that hurled back at her a vision. It flared through her, a wondrous display of cosmic ultimates. She lived with them as with old companions long gone, but always passionately loved in the heart beyond the conscious self.

She read, read greedily. Not that she rushed through the pages. Quietly, reverently she would take in the words. Only at times the flow of visions, the great upsurge of fire within her body would be so vehement, that her whole being would rebel madly at the slowness of the brain's response. She would read, read, eat up the pages with her mind, just feel, feel, not bother with clear cerebrations, but absorbing it whole, being drunken with ideas, drunken with the dream presence of Beings crowding around her, forcing her to welcome, forcing her to greet, to recognize, to be again what she was, what she ever is, one of them; beautiful, strong, radiant.

Boris cautioned her to be careful and go more slowly with her reading. He pointed out the danger of such a strong fare. The mind may burn itself into the frenzy of the revelation. Our bodies are not attuned to vibrations too metaphysical. As old contacts are made again, they overpower our present frame. It does not pay to be in a hurry. We must grow like plants. All stages are necessary from seed to stalk and flower and seed again.

She glowed with intense fervor. She seemed so light one was no longer conscious of her being an invalid. She seemed to soar and to dance with the winds. She was wings. She was fire. She burned into him who led her; through him she blazed forth. She was combustion. He was flame. There was light where they passed.

But light is hard to bear; light is death to the shadows in us and all others. Fire hollows out, even the most sublime. Where the radiance has been so rich, there comes the great darkness.

Boris left for the south. He was to be gone from three to four weeks. The few days that followed, she refused to admit his absence. Her love was too fundamentally impersonal to make a tragedy of mere bodily absence. She found him in the light that continued to flow from the books he had guided her through. She withdrew into the immanent shrine where their oneness had celebrated itself. She blinded herself to externalities. The within of trees and dust and stars sang the same booming tone of discovery.

spiritual flowering

Uncovered they were. All wrappings had glided away. The stark nakedness of all lives struck at her soul like a fanfare. It grew; it grew . . . until the roar of reality became a deafening cataract of truth. It glared at her. It took her and shook her. Her face hollowed. Her limbs trembled. Something poignant, unbearably beautiful seared her through. She refused to see anyone. She could not bear to see human faces. The bare reality of soul grinned at her behind the mask. She felt she was dissolving souls, violating them. She felt sacrilegious. Dazzling storms of light battered her mind.

One night, it gave up. She cried in delirium. She shouted incoherent words of ecstasy. "Mother! Mother! . . . all the snow . . . all the light. I am dancing; I am singing! Burn me. Boris! my Boris! . . . I am thy light. Hear me!" And she sang, full-voiced, exhilarated, with resonant, almost nonhuman tones. She could not be stopped. It was midnight. She sang through the night, then collapsed, moaning, still humming songs as if from beyond her exhausted body.

The doctor summoned could not find anything wrong organically. Perhaps a cerebral fever; she had burned herself out. Her nervous strength had collapsed. She slept for days afterwards. Hilda watched her day and night. She attended to her. She clung to her bed. The reflected flame of Rania's ecstasy seemed to have struck her at the heart. She was hanging to the sleeping one, as if entranced, haunted, in unrestrainable devotion.

Rania dreamt. Her dreams sang through her. Words rose from her like prayers. They rose like incense to him she loved, to the mystic being of whom he was but the shadow. They rang like incantations modulating strange names of other times. They quivered like gongs, rapturous and clear.

Hilda listened, tense like a resonating harp. The words struck at her and she trembled in tragic distress. As in a play of mirrors we see images inverted, so Rania's ecstatic love turned into bitter woe, into hatred in her convulsed mind. Yet she could not run away. She had to listen, to listen. She had to let the light eat her up like an acid. She could not escape it. She was bound to the light, irrevocably, pitilessly. She was bound to the illumined one, as a shadow to the tree, as reaction to action. She began to hate in the passionate fervor of love; to love in the desperate agony of hatred. She could not touch Rania's body without shivering with some excruciating pain of desire. Not even desire. She was past the stage of desiring anything, any gesture. She was wound up in Rania as the filament of moss in the resilient greens of redwoods and pines. To break away would be death, the multitudinous dying of the life-fibers, one by one torn, lacerated.

Mrs. Falkner at last understood. She had sensed tragedy seeping into Hilda's being. But she had too hermetically closed herself in her intellectual tower to escape and admit it. To admit it would have meant to become involved again in a world of pain she had hoped to shut out forever. Now however, the ominous attitude of her daughter had suddenly become too clear to be left unrecognized. One evening she happened to pass near the door of Rania's room which had been left half-unclosed. She stopped as she heard some strange spasmodic sobbing. She knew it was Hilda. In the dim light of a night lamp she saw Rania lying almost naked on her bed, apparently asleep, and Hilda kneeling, sob-broken, disheveled, her arms convulsed around the resting body, caressing, caressing passionately, yet not touching the flesh, not awakening, caressing with insane mumbling of words, poor haggard love words, shreds of hollowed heart, lacerating the silence with unbearable pain.

For a long time the wailing went on and the untactile quivering of hands and body. Then suddenly Rania moved, almost rose hardly awake. Hilda jumped to her feet, arranging distractedly the sheets.

"What is it, Hilda?"

"Oh! it was nothing. Just the sheets upset." She was fixing them for the night.

"I had a bad dream. I thought someone was piercing my entire body with sharp needles hidden in flowers . . . poisonous ones, it must have been. But I could not move . . . for the flowers were beautiful."

Hilda broke into desperate sobs.

"But, Hilda, why do you cry? Are you hurt?"

"Oh, no . . . not hurt. . . Just tired out." She must go to bed. She rushed out, not noticing her mother who had withdrawn in the darkness of an open door.

That night there was little sleep in the house. Mrs. Falkner's little world had cracked open like a frail crystal container. She was staring at it, helpless. What had really happened? How much of it could have come from Rania? How long had her poor little girl felt the hopeless desires? Or had it been a thing that had grown between them? Did Rania know it? She wondered what Boris would think, should he know. Perhaps he knew already. Perhaps he was not to come back. Then, what was she to do? Separate the girls? Travel? But she had no money. The only possibility would be for Hilda to go and resume her hospital work, far away; or else for Rania to go. How could it all be worked out without causing worse damage?

She suddenly realized how nervous and emaciated Hilda had

looked for weeks. She had thought it was just tiredness, the remains of a flu she had caught. But now she became aware of a deeper gangrene that corroded life from within. Not that she had any particular prejudice, or thought of immorality. She only saw Hilda waning away, eaten up by some unconquerable rust. She became frantic with the urge to save her. She ought to have known before. It was too late perhaps. Her life opened as a useless and miserable failure. She had endured moral agonies for this daughter of hers whom she wanted pure, beautiful, happy. She had tolerated the ordeal of conjugal cohabitation with a degenerate for Hilda's sake. Now she had let her waste herself away in an unnatural passion, unnoticed, carelessly. It was pitiful.

She arose. She wanted to go to Hilda's room, take her in her own arms, lull her tenderly, make her whole. She opened her door silently. She listened. There hung a heavy, unpeaceful silence, as in rooms whence sleep has departed. Darkness clings to the walls almost like black crepe, made more sinister yet by the bleak white corners of open windows. Oh, it was useless, Hilda could not understand. For a long time they had not been really intimate. It was hard for a mother to weave again tender feelings to cover the shivering soul of a daughter long estranged.

Rania heard her. She wondered. She felt a queer pressure around her heart, like that of impending disaster. She was stronger now. She felt stronger yet because of this sense of danger. It burst over her like a cold shower reviving her, shaking her from a long torpor. In sudden distress, her mind flew to Boris. Why was he not here? He had written but a couple of hasty notes. He was terribly busy, lecturing, seeing people, traveling through all the small towns of the southland, giving talks here and there, speaking above all about Russia and India to counteract the nefarious propaganda of newly published books and documents which were distorted accounts of conditions sufficiently difficult in themselves not to need such treatment. If she could only be with him! He had been right. She had overreached the goal, made a fool of herself in her uncontrollable fervor to know all and merge into great dangerous heights. Now, not only was she suffering from it, but Hilda, she realized, had been affected also; perhaps anxiety, sleeplessness—she was not sure. But she could see plainly upon her the marks of deep-seated tiredness, of intense nervous exhaustion.

Mrs. Falkner rose early. Hilda, after a dazed, empty night, one after many, had fallen asleep. Her mother heard her breathe, a little raw and strained, yet regular. She glided quietly downstairs and attended to the morning duties. Soon she was astonished to hear Rania moving in her room. She went to her. Was she getting up? Did she feel well again?

"Yes," said Rania. "I think I am quite all right. I just need to be careful, that is all. I have been a fool to concentrate so hard. I seem never to hit the midground. Always rushing madly ahead, as if I could force life. I suffer. Everybody suffers. It is ridiculous. Just when I thought I had come to a real sense of peace and destiny! Pfff! and here I am all up again!"

Mrs. Falkner helped her to dress. She stammered once or twice trying to unburden herself. She dared not. After all perhaps things were not as bad as she thought. Yet she managed to whisper: "I am worrying about Hilda. She looks absolutely worn out. I wonder what it is. I could not get her away from your bed, even when I was there and you were resting. There is something about her which is not natural. Do you feel it? Am I imagining things?"

"I know. She is not well." Rania answered slowly. She wondered what Mrs. Falkner really meant. She knew well Hilda's passionate devotion to her; it weighed upon her. She felt unfree, bound by strange creepers that held her prisoner, that oppressed her.

"Perhaps she ought to do some work again. She dreams too much. If she really studied something, it would be all right. But she only imagines, dreams. She is not fulfilled. She has not lived yet. She cannot stand it. I wish so much she could be healthy, like any other girl, court, marry! But she is afraid. What a dreadful thing, the fear of life!"

A moment later Hilda entered the room. She looked somewhat more rested; but her eyes flared like those of hasheesh eaters. They had no peace. They were craving to be ploughed by light, yearning to be fresh again, sun-lighted. Somehow Mrs. Falkner thought of her husband's look. She shuddered. Was it heredity? Was old blood fermenting in the child in spite of her love? But had she really loved her? Had she not been merely selfish, withdrawing from the girl when there was the greatest need for understanding and tenderness?

—∞◇∞—

A long letter came to Rania. Boris had been so much on the move that he had received no letter or news of any kind until then. Thus he had heard at the same time about her illness and her near-recovery. He begged her to relax and give her mind and nerves a chance to accustom themselves to certain changes that had happened within her. He suggested that it might be better either to see a great many people and have a plain good time or else to be alone as much as possible and lie on the grass and let telluric forces steady her disturbed and over-accelerated pulse. Anyway a change would be good for her if it were possible.

The letter seemed to crystallize a decision which had been forming slowly within her during the morning. She asked Mrs. Falkner if she could not go and stay all alone in a log-cabin which he and some friends had built quite a distance from Carmel beyond Point Sur. She felt the need for solitude and complete rest. Perhaps some friends could motor her down and arrange a few things around the cabin and make it easier. She would bring enough food for a week or two, and thus would have a marvelous rest far from books, human beings, and all strains.

Hilda thought it was a foolish plan. Why? She would die of boredom, and if anything happened to her whom could she call for help? But Mrs. Falkner was overjoyed with the suggestion. Such a change would do her much good. The air was warmer, drier there; the cabin was very comfortable and there was a farm nearby. She could arrange to have someone call for a moment every other day at least to see that she needed nothing. Hilda became sullen. Why could she not go also? She would not talk to her if she craved silence.

Rania shook her head. She took Hilda's hands and looked intently into the girl's unclear eyes.

"Hilda, why don't you start working again, and live your own life? You have been giving me all your time and care, and for that I am deeply, intensely grateful. But it is not right. I am well now. This thing that happened was purely mental and nervous. It is all over now. I am stronger and calmer than ever. I am facing a new life. You must face yours. You have lived with fear, as a recluse, shrinking from all that might have brought you joy, or at any rate experience—frightened by the mere possibility of sorrow and failure. That in itself is the greatest failure. It has brought disaster around you. Even now it blinds you."

Hilda laughed in answer. But her laughter was like the tones of a scarred bell. It was hollow and almost hoarse. She did not answer. Mrs. Falkner suggested she might phone the hospital about some nursing work. They had asked for her again a week ago, being very short of efficient help. Hilda began to tremble. Her face became white. What were they both plotting against her? They wanted to get rid of her? Why not say it plainly? She would not work in the hospital. She hated the thought of it. Rather waitress in a restaurant. She had seen too much of it while nursing Rania. She could not do it any longer. She could not stand the misery of it. How could they suggest it to her? If she was no longer wanted at home, all right, she would go, beg in the street! God! was that her recompense for having watched day and night over Rania, for having kept the house for her mother that she might pass hours plunged in her empty books? Why should she bother after all, fool that she was! If Rania wished to be sick at Point Sur and dream all alone of her prophet and god, why should she not? The pity of it! That was life. Afraid, was she? God! what was there to be more afraid of than those we thought we loved, parents, friends, all! She would not stand it. She could not go on. They had better leave her alone, alone . . . alone!

She ran upstairs sobbing hysterically, slammed the door of her room. They heard her fall over her bed which vibrated. Her mother stood up, aghast. She looked at Rania. Big tears were filling her eyes. There was a painful silence. Rania rose slowly on her crutches.

"You go and help her, Mrs. Falkner. It is better. I shall phone Peter Harbin and ask him to motor me down to the cabin. Tomorrow is Saturday. He will probably be able to do it. I must go . . . and leave you both. You have much to do together."

—∞◇∞—

spiritual flowering

CHAPTER V

The next day Rania left with Peter Harbin and his young sister, Nadia, who had recently come from boarding school to recover from illness. Their parents had been killed in Russia. She was seventeen. He was working for the newspaper, getting ads, interviewing people of importance drifting in or through Carmel. He was strangely quiet. Hardly ever spoke. He had seen too much perhaps.

His manners were refined. In this at least he remembered his aristocratic youth. The rest he had forgotten, deliberately. His family had fought with the whites. He hated the carnage, atrocities committed, the whole game of counter-revolution. A youth of twenty, he had fled with his little sister, worked his way through China, Japan; then San Francisco. Working as a clerk for a firm, he began to hate the city. His sister was alone, needed care. Someone mentioned Carmel. He hiked down the coast, carrying her in his arms part of the time. He had been there ever since. Having received some money from friends, he had sent Nadia to a girls' school in San Francisco, for the last three winters. But she hated it. She loved the sea, to run barefoot in the woods, to roll on the sand, to cut the breakers with her smooth bladelike body. Illness had been a good pretext. She would stay now in Carmel. She would wait in a tearoom and help her brother keep his little two-room cottage in the pinewoods.

Rania had seen her but twice since she had arrived. She began to love her tenderly. She recalled to her so much of her own youth, her own vigor, agility of old. They both came from neighboring lands. There was something of the same rich, free blood in them. It flared forth in contact with vast power-filled America. But in Nadia there was a curious reticence, a quiet simplicity that her elder had lacked. The child was meeting life on a more objective, more accurate, more dispassionate plane. She belonged to a colder generation; to one which estimates and analyzes more, which may run wild and fall into hectic depravations, but does so objectively, cold-bloodedly, with a queer mixture of experimental daring, sheepish desire to conform to what everyone does, and disabused boredom; yet with keen and vivid intuitions ready to pierce through shams and pathetic sentimental shells.

They sped on the precipitous road, making sharp turns over sheer cliffs. The hills now rose more majestically. They stretched up, fervently green, huge bodies lying parallel on their side, feet deep in the waters, heads toward the land, beyond. Dark canyons heavied with hairlike trees told mysterious pungent secrets. Brooks gurgled through, soon vanishing into the rock-strewn ocean. The magnificence of it was overwhelming. It dilated one into new dimensions, into some supernal kinship with elemental powers. From these limbed forms an intense vitality surged. They vibrated with power. Half-sunken gods and goddesses loved in tumultuous embraces.

That love grew more heroic still, yet more serene, as the coast unfolded, as Point Sur was left behind and new perspectives, bent to the southeast, arose under paling skies. Opalescent mist floated at the confine of sea and land. The road mounted up, leaving the waters below, high over fog. The blue expanse of sea grew vertical. The earth heaved still more majestic curves that struck the ocean in a magnificent sweep. Torso piled over torso in cosmic slumber. The air felt warmer, more lucent. It glowed with the rising moon, a seed thrown upward from the meeting of earth and sea. This moon seemed to bring the whole vision to a focus. It made the mist iridescent, which the last sun-glow licked from below. All curves became transfixed by the red spear of light that sank far away in the unknown.

On a rounded eminence, commanding all the coast north and south, the log cabin stood, placid and low. Nadia jumped from the car before it stopped. She could not stand still. The power of the earth boiled through her. She was drunken with being flung open at the sky. She kissed the sturdy oaks, spirals of strength radiating from the hills, locks of dark curly hair with grasping roots, tense fiber and brittle leaves. Rania breathed deeply the marvelous scent and ecstasy of the winds that were blowing and surging. The moment was so strong, she feared it would break from too much intensity. She closed her eyes to feel it deeper. She thought of Boris. How she wanted him here! His spirit would feel akin to the grandeur of the earth. It would mount the earth as a pedestal to cry out from their bare summits, dome of fecundity, the tone of rising ages, of the new child of regenerated manhood.

The night grew colder. Logs burned and crackled in the huge fireplace. The flames danced, wondrous release from the rigidity of the wood. They, too, were life-cries surging from huge trunks that had grown silently for centuries. From the very death of the trees there came now dancing tones, leaping incandescence, warmth that one stretches into, that one breathes in with open lungs; good warmth.

—∞◇∞—

Nadia and Peter slept out of doors. They wanted to be wax for the immensity, wax for it to stamp itself upon during the emollient hours of sleep. They were up early. The sun was warm; the south wind blew them fragrances that seemed to remember orange fields and sagebrushes. Hours of deep inbreathing passed. They went swiftly by. Nadia looked at Rania with tear-heavied eyes when her brother mentioned departure. She did not dare ask in words; but her entire being implored. Rania understood. There was so much happiness flowing from earth to humans and back to the earth, that she was afraid to break the contact. Her eyes said "yes" before her lips shaped the word.

Then she remembered Hilda had asked her to go with her and might feel hurt if Nadia would remain. The thought shot through her just as Nadia threw herself on her neck, kissing her with joyful excitement. It was too late, now, to refuse. Peter left alone. He was to come back for them in two weeks, unless they would send word before. As he left, Rania felt some dark wing graze her. A poignant hurt stopped her heart. She stood, wondering. Nadia was looking toward the sea. Her strong yet slender body profiled itself against the sun illumining from below the full underfoliage of the oaks. It seemed to take hold of the youth and lift her heavenward. Light claimed her. Nadia stretched her arms for some great wing-flight. The sun owned her. As she turned suddenly crying out in rapture: "Rania, look!" the light seemed to throw her at Rania's face. Behind her one could observe, faintly lighted, the evening star.

Then passed days of pure and serene felicity. The fresh open wonders of the young girl produced a strange exaltation in Rania.

spiritual flowering

She communed again through her with radiant life. In most beings she could always sense a tension, a bruised unwholesome feeling, or else a sort of excited forgetfulness, like grownups trying to become as children. The ego stood up in most of them like huge signs in public parks: "Do not trespass," or "Private Property" along country roads.

Nadia glowed with the openness of an everlasting: "Come through me." She was amazingly unselfconscious. She knew she was there. It was she herself, Nadia. Nobody had any business to spoil that; and her mind was very clear about what that meant. She was not going to lose her head. She was quietly passing through life; therefore life and all living things were welcome to pass through her. Quietly—but a strange intoxicated quiet. A great inner certitude which could afford to be passionately disturbed. She was so sure of knowing, that she was perfectly at ease in ignorance. That was the reason she hated school. They tried to teach her what she knew she knew somewhere. She did not bother much to find out where this somewhere was. Like so many modern youths, she was a fatalist. She sensed the absurdity of her elders' bragging vanity of self. She saw clearly and calmly the mess they had made of their own lives. The older generation came for judgment before her absolutely unsentimental clear-sightedness. The figure it made was so grotesque and their big words so childish, that she could not refrain from a sort of generalized smile of pity. They were all right, the poor dears! They would know some day.

At first Rania was a little taken aback by such an attitude. Then she realized that it really was at the bottom of the extravagances and apparent cold conceit of modern youth. She felt it justified, even if it was only a half-wisdom, and a rather disconcerting sort of wisdom at that. It seemed to complement in a subtle way her own tempestuous sense of selfhood and her strained fervor. It was true that she had always opened herself to life and felt an inner certainty beyond her turmoils; but there was a difference. It was herself, Rania, that opened herself and was certain. But in a curious way she felt in her companion not Nadia-the-open, but openness-called-Nadia; a subtle reversal, impersonality of a kind, with a coloring of extreme personality on the surface. Objectivity *was*, where, in Rania, subjectivity had yearned. Only recently could she feel herself really objectively peaceful, poised in destiny. In Nadia destiny was splashing into personality; but underneath the iridescent foam, the waters of life flowed, strong, unmoved, clear.

Every day Nadia went, alone, for long walks over the hills, through the canyon filled with decaying trunks and colossal redwoods, rust-eaten in many places, yet stubbornly darting through the thicket, sky-intoxicated. She came back, hot and disheveled, glowing. She would lead Rania to the cliff's edge. Then with sure agility she would run down steep paths to the sea. She would throw her clothes away, and shouting to Rania who could hardly hear her voice from her three- or four-hundred-foot elevation, would jump into the cold waves. Then, wet and salty, half-wrapped, she would climb the nearly perpendicular cliffs, and throw herself into Rania's arms, a thing of the sea, effervescent with foam and wind.

Before the fire they talked. Rania had felt her way carefully into her mysterious intangible openness. She had found where the open closed into a soul-womb, in which she began to rouse the deeper sense of spiritual motherhood, the sense of the sacredness of ideas, the sense of racial duty, or self-dedication. Nadia began to feel the restriction of a destiny. It gave a meaning to her certainty; it made it become human. From elemental openness and instinctual stability to human meaningfulness, the road may be hard and tragic. It often needs to be tragic with most of our youth whose hectic sophistication answers to the grotesque hypocrisy of their elders. But where the elders can guide the younger ones into selfhood and the sense of destiny, there may come quick and wondrous growth and the descent of soul into the open vase.

Dreams came to Rania. Their fringes of reality bore heavily upon her consciousness. They seemed to flow in two layers, one very sombre, oppressed by the insistent beating of some outer sea upon her soul petrified into some mysterious stone-duty; the other, intense with unremembered events of some far-distant beyond, out of which she would feel only Boris's face emerging transfigured by an unearthly radiance. These two dream worlds lived with her all through the day in an occult polyphony, the harmony of which was evident, yet intensely dissonant. The physical world seemed to act as a unifier, the two streams to converge in this waking mind that almost collapsed under the stress of the harmonization.

But when the pressure was greatest Nadia would always appear from nowhere apparently, and her presence would act as a tonic, focusing the tensions into a definite orb. These tensions would knead themselves into a stream of power that would rush into what would appear as the vacuum of Nadia's soul, there to take form and virtue. And Rania would witness herself in young sun-streaming eyes that loved her. Was it a mysterious transfer of power, of destiny? They both felt it as a sacred rite that was being celebrated in and through them. It made hours and days sing paeans of deliverance and fecundation.

—∞◇∞—

Peter came two days before the expected time. It happened that he appeared unnoticed as Nadia had run half-clad from her ocean bath up the long winding path and was lying close to Rania on the grass, trying to regain her breath. As Rania turned quickly in hearing footsteps and threw a blanket over the half-naked girl, she saw Peter's face turn sullen and strained.

"Oh! it is you, Peter! We did not expect you so soon. Nadia has just come back from her bath. She is still out of breath."

Yes, he had come sooner, being unexpectedly free and thinking he would enjoy a day or two of rest with them. Rania asked a little anxiously about Mrs. Falkner and Hilda. Peter answered evasively. They were not very well. Hilda had apparently taken a great fancy to Robert Johnson; they were much together. But she seemed terribly nervous, and her mother very depressed.

He brought several letters for Rania. Two were from Boris whose coming was to be once more delayed by new engagements around San Francisco. These were to be positively the last, however. He was weary of continuous talking, of being always on the go with people. The plan for his big book had come to a definite point of crystallization in his mind. He had decided to start writing it at once—this would mean many months of quiet work. Carmel seemed the proper place, and the thought of being with her again and of relaxing into creative work elated him intensely.

Another letter was from her lawyer. Her husband's father had fought stubbornly against giving her any more money after Richard's death, and only after many threats of lawsuits had he proposed to pay her the round sum of a few thousand dollars—a small amount in view of his wealth—which her lawyer urged her to accept. Her house in the Hollywood canyon was about to be sold for a good price, and she would thus have a capital, the income of which would be sufficient for her needs.

The morning after, while Nadia was away hiking, Peter, whose reserved attitude had somewhat disconcerted Rania, asked her to give him a few moments for a talk which he felt was necessary, however unpleasant it might be. "What was it?" she asked. She was ready for the worst.

Well, it had happened like this. When he had come back after leaving them both, he had received the next morning a visit from Hilda, who had asked how Rania was. Of course he had told her that Nadia had stayed with Rania. Upon hearing this Hilda had turned terribly white, had almost collapsed; then after recovering herself, had flown in a sort of hysterical rage, swearing at him, insulting him for leaving his sister in the hands of a woman who was perverse and corrupt, who had attempted many times to seduce her and make love to her. He was a big fool. Did he not know what kind of creature Rania was? He should look at her, Hilda; for months she had slaved at her side nursing her. In recompense she had gotten what? Mistreatment and obscene propositions. Now, she was a nervous wreck. She had wanted to take a rest and go to Big Sur. But no, Rania would have nothing of her. Rania wished to be alone, to meditate, to dream of her god, Boris. Nonsense! What she wanted was to lay hands upon a young girl and satisfy her lust. God! what a pity the whole thing was!

Then Hilda had almost collapsed and he had to carry her back to her mother. At first he did not know what to believe. The accusation seemed to him monstrous. Yet there must be something wrong somewhere. It was his duty to find out somehow something of the truth. Well, he had wanted first to come back at once to Big Sur. But he decided to have a talk with Mrs. Falkner. It had been a painful one. The woman almost broke down on hearing even the few guarded words he had said in order to feel the ground. She had told him she suspected Hilda of being terribly in love with Rania. She had seen some things which had opened her eyes suddenly. She did not think Rania was at fault. Yet she could not tell for sure. She was broken by the whole thing.

Hilda had suddenly turned to Robert, the poor boy who had been in love with her for months. She had thrown herself at him in a sort of unnatural, hectic way, and Mrs. Falkner felt that nothing but catastrophe could possibly come from such an outburst. She was sure Hilda did not love him, but did it all out of spite and rancor. The situation was becoming unbearable. She thought Rania had better not live with them any longer; yet she hated to see her alone.

After that he had thought he would wait a little before coming back to Big Sur and see how things would develop. He had not heard anything more; but he had come ahead of time to be able to talk to her and ask her frankly to tell him on her word of honor what had been the matter between her and Hilda. Not that he especially cared to know her own private matters; but his sister's name, reputation and happiness were involved and while he had trusted Rania and did not come back at once to take away his sister, still things did not look too clear. He felt he had the right to know, under his own pledge of secrecy.

Rania had kept very still during the long speech. Her face had become quite drawn and stonelike. The outer darkness was pounding upon it. She had to be calm, quiet. Was it not her task to stand and remain, resisting with stoic indifference the impact of the destructive winds, sheltering the seeds within the great wall of protection? Yet her mind worked intensely. It dug into the past, flew over the plains of futurity. It weighed causes and effects. It evaluated the possible reactions of denials, affirmations, concealment. It tried to read Peter's thoughts, deeper still, his heart. How much did he believe? How much would he understand of the truth, if told? How much of it would help him, help her, and above all Nadia? For the one great thought in her, that which rang foremost, louder than her own sense of honor, or truthfulness, of anything whatsoever, was: to save Nadia from trouble, from the destruction of the new inner beauty that had begun to develop within her and which brutal incriminations or suspicions might suddenly shatter.

And so she turned her eyes toward Peter and holding them straight and deep into his own, she said very quietly, yet with vibrant intensity:

"What Hilda told you is *not* true, Peter. And you can be sure that your sister has not heard a word from me or seen any gesture which might have conveyed to her any feeling or desire from my part which would not have been pure and natural. I have found in her a beautiful younger sister; and I love her as such. And we have had wonderful talks and rich days. I believe she discovered in me things that none of her young friends at school had been able to give her. There is nothing at all that can be open to reproach, I swear to you.

"As to Hilda, I am deeply sad and pained to see her in such a condition. I felt she would be jealous knowing that Nadia was staying with me. But I had already told your sister she could remain. Even though I thought Hilda might be somewhat hurt, I never would have believed she would throw herself into such a state of madness and hysteria. She was wonderful to me when I was so terribly ill and helpless. Her devotion has been amazing. Well, Peter, you can imagine how close our contacts have been. She has handled my body for months. She has done everything for me. Of course it was done professionally. She was paid for it all the time I was in the hospital and even for a while after. I have been paying my board in Mrs. Falkner's home all the time. These are trivial matters, but you must know so that you will not get a wrong impression of me.

"I have known or suspected for a long time that Hilda's attachment for me was much too personal, even physical. I had no repulsion from it, but I did not encourage it. I thought the girl was high-strung and I urged her all the time to be with boys and live a natural life, instead of being in constant fear of life. What else could I do? Perhaps I should have left the house. But then Boris came into my life. I did not want to precipitate anything. She became jealous of Boris, too, it seems. Perhaps the intensity of my devotion to his work and his wisdom has generated energies which have reacted upon Hilda in a destructive way. I really cannot know fully. I have been ill and delirious for a few days. Something may have happened which I have not been conscious of. I know Mrs. Falkner has been very upset ever since. What did she see? I do not know. She did not tell me. I can only affirm that I have not been conscious of anything in which I had any guilt whatsoever.

"You may not believe me. I suppose that if Hilda goes on telling such a story about me, people will believe her. I cannot do anything about it. Can I? I only hope it will not reach Nadia's ears. For while I suppose she understands these things, as all our youngsters seem to, yet it might disturb her and have a bad effect upon her.

"And now, tell me, what shall we do about it?"

Obviously there was nothing to be done, Peter answered. He was glad to have heard what she had said. He was willing and happy to believe her and he would watch for any possible development. In the meantime he did not know whether it might not be best for her to leave the Falkner house.

"But," said Rania, "if I do suddenly, Hilda may become still more jealous and circulate more infamies concerning my relation to Nadia."

spiritual flowering

There was the problem. She thought she had to go back first to the Falkners, and see how things would turn out. Rushing any decision might make matters worse.

—∞◇∞—

The return to Carmel was somewhat sullen and tense. Nadia noticed a certain serious air about her companions, and she wondered silently what the reason for it might be. She would have to find out. Rania tried to be gay, but somehow it did not ring very true; and Nadia's big eyes would look into hers questioningly. Would she have the courage to carry on the comedy? She had the uncomfortable feeling that Peter was watching more or less unconsciously their every move. It made gestures tense and somewhat forced.

Rania returned home. Mrs. Falkner welcomed her with sad, worn-out sleepless eyes. Hilda was driving with Robert Johnson. They had suddenly become inseparable. Tired with the trip, Rania went to bed. She slept badly. Hilda came in late, slammed the doors, as if purposely. Rania heard her through the thin partition, sighing, speaking incoherent words in dreams. When at last she herself slumbered she passed from one nightmare to another. She felt oppressed. Her body ached. The air was damper in Carmel. Rain was coming again. A great darkness overwhelmed her which grew thicker as dawn came, as she again met Hilda, whose face seemed to be brave with an air of bitter defiance, as she talked alone to Mrs. Falkner about the situation created by Hilda's behavior. Robert Johnson was running around all day with her. He was almost giving up his job in Monterey. People had begun to talk about it. What could be done to avert more tragedy?

Rania decided to leave the house. Hilda shrugged her shoulders when told. All right! If she had had enough of them, why not try

RANIA

someone else! Rania took a room in the La Fonda Hotel. She
thought it would be wiser than to rent a cottage. Her actions
would lead less to misinterpretations, and besides, she would have
service and would feel less lonely.

But rain set in for a week of continuous downpour. The streets
were torrents. Roofs leaked. Rheumatic pains, sciatica took hold
of her. She was soon confined to her bed in great pain. Hilda did
not come to see her. Nadia was busy in a tearoom and managed to
steal but a few moments to visit Rania who did not dare urge her
to come too often.

Days of terrible depression weighed drearily upon the brave soul
upon whom destiny was beating relentlessly. Boris wrote a few
words of cheer that stirred her. What would he say? She would tell
him all. He knew already perhaps. What would he think of Nadia?
He must love her, help her. Boris—Nadia. These were her two
lights that kept flaming forth. Yet she had almost ceased to care.
All was the same. Nothing mattered much. She was so weary. She
could no longer stand physical pain. She begged for morphine. It
calmed her. She began to dream. She did not want food. The fog
and rain pressed in. The drops of water hit the house's skull and
fever grew all around. It pounded the silence. It shrieked
agonizing counterpoints on the bass of the sea, on the wails of the
wind, shaking the pines as one shakes a drunkard to bring him to
his senses. The Big Sur days stood out, golden mosaic of dreams in
a haunted decrepit church filled with bats.

Nadia herself seemed rain-beaten. She had dimly sensed what had
happened. She had asked Rania cautiously. Rania did not say
much, but enough to open the girl's eyes. Nadia had never liked
Hilda. She sensed that Rania suffered from things Hilda had said;

152

spiritual flowering

she guessed what it must have been. It depressed her. A beautiful
fire that had blazed forth was dying now in the dark. She felt cold,
shivering, damp. She grew vindictive toward her brother.

In the midst of this distress, there came to Carmel a man who called
himself Sarmananda.

—◦◇◦—

sacrifice
of the seed

CHAPTER I

Sylvia Rutherford had met Sarmananda in London. At that time she was dabbling in ceremonial magic and the Kabbalah. She had been suddenly frightened by the strange and seemingly related deaths of two of the men who seemed to have attained proficiency in the weird operations. In each case doctors had diagnosed a sudden rupture of the heart. On one of the bodies autopsy had been performed, since the man had had a strong physique and there had been no hint of heart disease. It was discovered that the heart had been suddenly torn or rather pierced as if with a sharp sword. Yet there had been no bodily injury. The case had somewhat puzzled the physicians. Overstrain, they declared. But Sylvia had been lucid enough to connect these deaths with occult practices and the use of ceremonial swords. Stricken with a sort of panic, she had looked around almost frantically for help and salvation.

Sarmananda was introduced to her. He was supposed to be an exponent of Buddhism. He claimed that officially known Buddhism was but the shell of the living doctrine of Gautama. He was expounding teachings which, in their practical as well as metaphysical aspects, were supposed to effect the regeneration of the individual and lead to a harmonized state of perfection and identification with the world-energy. In fact his doctrine was a queer mixture of subtle psychology, of metaphysical Buddhism as taught in some North Indian schools, and of more or less disguised Tantrik practices. He had, of course, "esoteric" as well as exoteric teachings. The former dealt definitely with the arousal of bodily energies. The body, he said, was the microcosm. It was so linked with the macrocosm or universal being that by acting on the former the latter could be reached. Nirvana was a condition of equilibration. If it could be induced in the body through proper contemplation, objectification and harmonization of energies, then it would free the individual consciousness linked with that body, and cosmic consciousness would follow.

Cosmic consciousness, fourth dimension, equilibration were magical words for many. Weary of their own selfhood and of their own body, they sought release in the promised land of a mysticism, the entrance to which seemed within easy reach of those complying with certain rules and performing exercises which, at first, seemed healthy and attractive. The sudden death of American relatives had, however, forced Sylvia to leave London and her teacher after a few weeks of contact. Circumstances had so shaped themselves that she remained in America. Having heard that Sarmananda was touring the States, delivering lectures to crowded halls in many big cities, she had written him urging him to come for at least a few days to Carmel. He had come.

Rumors of his San Francisco lectures were exciting. He seemed to have a great sway over his public. He spoke in abrupt, forceful tones. The regenerate consciousness: that was his great theme. "Make your body cosmic and you become the Infinite Mind." A subtle dialectic cemented his entire doctrine into a fascinating whole for men who wanted to find God here and now. He knew American psychology, its trend toward behaviorism, toward practical efficiency, its craving for health, bliss, optimism. "Why be ill, why be limited?" he thundered forth. "You *are* the whole here and now. Why don't you know it? Because you are polarized; only half of your own self. Equilibrate yourself, develop your other hidden self. Contemplate the hidden face of the moon in yourself. Then eternity will be yours. No one can help you but yourself. Free your consciousness from this half-body of yours. If you watch all your actions, all your functions with intense awareness, as Buddha bid his disciples do," he claimed, quoting texts, "if you examine your own chemicalizations and rhythms of living, then little by little the hidden half of yourself will begin to appear to you. Do not be afraid of it. It may seem a strange and fantastic shape. But keep watching and you will see its shadows complement your known highlights. And you will grow into wholeness."

Sarmananda was tall and powerfully built. His dark eyes glowed with a strange yellowish light. They were half-veiled save in moments of vehemence, when the eyelids would suddenly open and an uncanny energy would flow from the spotted globes underneath a protruding forehead. There was power in him, but a sort of tense sinister power. When Rania saw and heard him she shivered and said to Nadia, who recoiled instinctively from the man: "He may be whole, but it must be from eating up the rest of the world!"

Nadia assented and nicknamed him "the Ogre."

However Carmel flocked to his lectures. He had a keen psychological sense and transformed his teachings to suit the needs and prejudices of his audiences. He was very intellectual, logical, psychological. He portrayed the many functions of the body, showed where they set traps for the consciousness which always longed to be active and to flow into the very organs it should only use as instruments. The task was to set this consciousness, this "I," free by creating balancing counter-rhythms. He was not very explicit as to how it was to be done. The processes had to be watched carefully. A teacher was necessary in most cases; personal directions for practical work were required.

The inference was clear. He could but promulgate the philosophy to a large audience; the practice of contemplation, self-watchfulness and bodily analysis was relatively a simple one. But the deliberate attempt to set counter-rhythms required the guidance of one who knew. Besides, it necessitated group work in order to be fully worked out. The process of equilibration had to be stimulated by an interplay of magnetisms of different types.

To Rania it was evident that the latter theory would lead to some form of sex magic. But at first when asked to give her opinion on Sarmananda, she answered evasively. To her, he was not sympathetic, but it might be only a personal reaction. She was in passionate eagerness to see Boris and talk to him about the Hindu. She wrote him letters entreating him to come at once. She felt some sinister influence whirling around poor frantic souls who were sincerely, but oh! how foolishly and hectically, searching for some peaceful haven. Now a powerful man had come and they rushed toward him in excited worship.

Rania was not well yet. Darkness seemed to have become positive and taken anchorage. It was grinning silently, as if saying: "I am waiting. My time will come. I shall have you all." At night it took form almost; a grimacing, monstrous shape that hovered over Carmel. The huge column of blackness rose from the Point, close to Lobos. It stood. It watched. Rania saw it grow toward the sky. She was helpless. She was a puny thing in front of the huge mass. But the horror of the face she could sense within the mass froze her heart; and she would wake up shivering yet perspiring.

Days passed like nightmares. Nadia ran to her as often as she could. She, too, felt nearly lost, frightened to be alone. Her brother seemed much interested in Sarmananda. He liked the keen psychological analysis of the teacher, his objectivity and impassibility. Nadia had tried to contradict him and got furious telling him what a fool he was making of himself being taken in by "the Ogre." Peter had sneered at her, asking her sharply to stop her childish pranks. She had bitten her lips not to answer. But she felt dreadfully unhappy. Something would have to happen. Thank God, she would be eighteen in a few weeks and no one had better try to boss her then.

Hilda and Robert, more inseparable than ever, had become, with Sylvia and a few others, assiduous worshipers at the Hindu's shrine. They were beginning to form a group for private instruction. Mrs. Falkner was hesitating. Her mind seemed suddenly to reel. A terrible bitterness possessed her. She distrusted everybody. She hardly saw Rania any more. She hardly saw anyone. She looked ghastly, aged almost beyond recognition.

March storms had come. They tore through the trees. They lashed. They spread a bitter taste of foam over all living things. Point Lobos was shaken by the furious impacts of the sea. Peter drove Rania to the peninsula's end where the sea tides clash in vertical thunder. A raw, biting wind forced its way through clothes, walls, bedsheets. It claimed domination. It froze one to the marrow. Rania shivered. Her legs and arms were nearly paralyzed with neuritis. She tucked herself in woolens; electric pads hardly could warm her thin blood. Her eyes seemed to have sunk into rigidity and forced silence. She came back from the drive worse than ever. She had felt a change in Peter. He was getting more excitable. She thought he had heard more stories about herself. Or was it

Sarmananda's influence? She had been but two or three times to the lectures. But when drawn into an unwelcome introduction to him and forced to shake his hand, she had felt an awful repulsion and had withdrawn precipitately. She had seen a disconcerted, then penetrating, then angry and sarcastic look in his eyes. When she had come to the other lectures, she had felt his glance heavy upon her. She had shuddered, had tried to compose herself and to send him as much love and gentle compassion as she could marshal. But disgust had overwhelmed her. She had left hurriedly while people pressed around the great man, gathering into his orb as fascinated moths.

Sarmananda left to fill engagements in the south. But he promised to come back the following year and gave fuller instructions to Sylvia who, mainly with the help of Hilda and Robert, was to hold a small group together. They were to meet twice a week in the evening. What they actually did was meant to be secret. They were "growing into wholeness" through their bodies! Soon after, a curious look began to creep over their faces, a strained look. Hilda especially appeared almost haggard. She hardly spoke to Rania, even when she met her in public; or else she greeted her with ostensible affection.

Boris, who had been fully informed by Rania's letters of the situation, was to come back a couple of days later. He had met Sarmananda once or twice in the east, and a few weeks before, in San Francisco. He did not hesitate in denouncing his teachings to Rania as a dangerous perversion of what he thought the true doctrine; doubly dangerous they were, since Sarmananda used terms and ideas which outwardly and in the context he gave them sounded exactly like the true spiritual ones, thus misleading people, confusing their minds and at the same time discrediting the true philosophy in the eyes of those who had tasted of the

sacrifice of the seed

Hindu's practical teachings and had realized their eventual consequences.

—∞◇∞—

In the evening Boris arrived.

Peter rode to Monterey and brought him from the station to the Lincoln Inn where he took a room; then to Rania. No, he would not stay. They would want to talk alone and he was very busy. Rania was lying on her sofa, still in great pain. But her arms flew to the beloved as desert winds at night to the sea. How she had longed for him! He bowed over her, gently, lovingly he kissed her forehead. She had suffered so much. He had felt it beating upon him from afar. Many a time he came near leaving everything and rushing to her. He had to fulfill his destiny. Now, he was free. Nothing could take him from the work he wanted to accomplish in Carmel. Was she not in this work? She had fought bravely, he knew. They must work together, make a record of truth; yes, even here, where so much falsehood and dismal darkness was being concentrated. It was always from the deepest pits that the flame must rise. They would live and record the great cosmic truth of which Carmel was the planetary altar, where the shadow of this truth was most somber. Were there not small cottages near Lobos, or in the Highlands where he could work quietly—where perhaps she would come also and stay?

She looked at him with big, solemn eyes.

That would be another scandal . . . if they were to live together. Who would understand? No, he shook his head, not necessarily scandal. He knew the whole situation. Rania had written him enough already, and Mrs. Falkner had said in her two or three letters all that was needed to complete the story. He would not add

163

one more disturbance to an already complex situation. He had thought it all out. She needed protection. And if she was willing to consider it in the spirit in which he was contemplating the action, he saw no reason why they should not give to their sacred companionship, as co-devotees of the same ideal, as communicants in the same dedication to the selfless service of humanity, the social appearance of a legalized union. It would not, could not, be obviously what men call a marriage. His life no longer belonged to him. Perhaps her own life also was no longer her own. But behind the useless social form they would be sheltered; the work would be sheltered. It might mean sacrifice on her part. He had practically nothing but himself to offer—in a sense, not even that—only a new opportunity for service, a further consecration, a deeper abnegation. Yet he had to ask her. She need not answer now.

She looked at him with big solemn eyes.

She took his hands, pressed them into acquiescence.

No, she did not need to think it over. It was all thought over, long ago. She had dreamt he would come and ask her. She had dreamt they would both fight as soldiers in the great struggle, hand in hand—as she now pressed his hands; a chain of power. She had seen the darkness crowd up on her, not being able to reach her, for the time had not come yet. There was work to be done. She knew herself necessary. What was she to bring to it? She did not know—a renunciation perhaps. Her broken helpless body might not stand the strain much longer. But while it would keep up, she would be game, would do her work—with him. She understood now what work meant, and utter loyalty to that work in complete self-denial. She realized that here on this plane there was one thing needed: activity. To fulfill one's function in activity, in dispassionate selfless activity; that was all. But not being attached to the fruits of action. Not being attached, not binding others either.

sacrifice of the seed

Being free because refusing to be a master of slaves. Being free.
Two free beings, many free beings, many companions. Oh! how
could she hesitate? She was ready for all sacrifices, for all deepest
consecrations—if need be alone, in sorrow and distress; but
happily, joyously, in great boundless love, with him.

Her hands pressed his hands in affirmation.

Affirmation of purpose, of a truth.

There was nothing in her he could not see; she would lay herself
open and bare, transparent. She had struggled. She had failed many
times perhaps. But she had clung to one central faith, to one
ultimate reality within. Now that she was able to see her past
unfolding in cyclic tides, she could better grasp the sense of it all,
the sense of the realization which was to be hers, in death or
rebirth. She had been surrounded by deaths. She had caused them
unwillingly. She was a power that seemed to have the fatality of
burning many. She had not known how to wield that power, how
to attenuate the flame in compassion for the weak. That had been
her selfishness. It had become clear to her. She had burned herself
up, in burning others. But out of that fatality something had to
grow. She had to bequeath a trust, a legacy. To whom? To what?
She began to perceive it all. But words were of little use in such
matters. He would know. He knew perhaps already. She had
craved nobility of soul. She had yearned for noble men and women
who could sound forth the great tone of this heroic strenuous age
of spiritual wars. She had longed to mother a little body into such
a consummation. But she was not to be a mother of bodies. Yet
she might have herself to bequeath. One can truly give in sacrifice
only what one is. Well, she was ready. Affirmation of a will, of a
truth.

The following day Nadia met Boris.

She had come to Rania to bring her flowers, eager to know the outcome of her meeting with Boris. She had heard so much about him that she was almost afraid to see him. Rania did not say much; she wanted her to know Boris before she would announce their contemplated union. She phoned him to come if he could. As he entered the room Nadia rose, nervously. She withdrew a little. She knew already so strongly from within that all she could say or do was meaningless—that all was implicitly done and said, and that this meeting of bodies was a mere formality—that it almost frightened her. She could but draw very close to Rania and stand, silent. "Boris, this is Nadia"; she heard the words. She sensed herself stretching a hand that met a stronger one. Then she was no more. Something happened that annihilated her. Words were exchanged; they seemed meaningless. She stood helplessly trying to be a self again. As Rania called her, she moved toward the couch. Rania drew her close, pressed her into her arms. She saw Boris smile; with deep poignant tenderness something leaped forth in her breast that made her cry. She kissed Rania foolishly, childishly. She laughed. There was someone else in her. It felt so strange. She was all distended; not open, but distended almost infinitely. She tasted the sun and the ocean inside of her. All things around looked funny, transparent. What had happened?

That day Nadia met Boris.

Rania told her she would live with him.

Nadia looked at her, questioning . . . at Boris who was watching her intently.

Yes, they had decided that for the sake of the work and of their very friends, they would go through the usual marriage ceremony as simplified as possible, and so establish a social basis for their activities which otherwise might suffer from all that obviously would be said. Nadia seemed a little puzzled. It all came at once; and her world seemed suddenly so upset that she could not place things where she was accustomed to seeing them. They extended now so far beyond their old boundaries, disconcertingly far. Still, yes, of course, she was happy for it. She would always be glad of what made Rania happy. And, too, it seemed a logical thing to do. Then she burst out laughing. Oh! if she could only see Hilda's face when she would hear it! Rania frowned sadly. Hilda! poor Hilda. Nadia ought not to laugh about her. She was so miserable. Perhaps she would feel still more jealous, still more bitter. Boris said he would go himself that day to the Falkners.

He would announce his future marriage.

—∞◇∞—

In a few hours all Carmel knew.

Reactions were varied. Undermeanings were attributed. Some spoke in hushed voice of occult work that both had to do, with no idea at all of what this work might be, just babbling words to show off the depth of their own knowledge. Others laughed; well, after all Boris was a man just like any other! One or two insinuated that Rania had a good income, which might explain things a little. Hilda sneered contemptuously when her mother told her, after Boris had come to the house: "She has gotten him, at last! Well, I wonder what kind of a wife she will be! She was pretty helpless when I was not around." Mrs. Falkner shook her head sadly. "I think it is fine of Boris. The poor girl is suffering very much. It will be a blessing to her. She probably will be happy. After all she has passed through, she needs a little peace."

"Oh! yes, she needed peace indeed!" retorted Hilda. Boris would have a hard time to give it to her! She was selfish, that was all. She made everyone serve her. Now she had Boris in her net. And it would be interesting to watch the results. She could swear Boris would be ruined, like she was nearly ruined slaving for her. . . Her bitter words went on and on, to everyone who cared to hear her.

In a few hours all Carmel knew.

Legal procedures were soon over.

They bought a new car. Nadia drove them around to find a cottage. She was happy. She had accepted the situation joyfully. Bitterly she fought back depreciating comments which the Sarmananda group circulated. She even had a fight with her brother. Peter admired Boris. He thought the marriage was engineered as a way of clearing Rania's reputation, yet he could not help having suspicions. He wanted to know whether Rania and his sister had really not been guilty of too close an intimacy. He tried to say a few words here and there as soundings. Somehow Nadia felt he was driving at her. She was a child no longer. She flew into a rage, and swore she would leave the room instantly if he did not apologize. Taken aback, he withdrew. He was not convinced. Nadia began to hate him. Outside of her work hours she fled to Rania and Boris as to a refuge. There she glowed forth with joyous affirmation. Great happiness. A seed into the decaying humus.

In a few days they found a house.

Huge cliffs, rock edges sharpened by the impact of the sea. Pines with sturdy roots clamped in stone crevices. Where there was soil, grass and wildflowers by myriads; lupins bepurpled the strained outlines of the earth. Small creeks, with mystery hung around, trying to tell secrets, unfolding dreams of strange adventures; a few grottos. On the farther rocks, immersed in ever-churning waves, seals moved in pathetic incessant contortions. Huge sea worms, they seemed like grotesque attempts of life to glide slimily out of the waters. The first birth toward light; a tragic helpless struggle. The things of the sea were stunned by the sun and winds. They barked; they laughed monstrously. They clamored with the impotency of being at the mad sea gulls shrieking demonic sneers at the sloth of the things below. Toward the north, Lobos spearing the waves; south, the hills rose, majestic and solemn, heaving flowers and scented earth.

Carmel Highlands.

The cottage was spacious, comfortable.

Rania loved it so much she made up her mind to buy it with the money that had come to her from the settlement with her father-in-law. It was a good bargain. Land values were increasing. It would be a place where no one could dispute their right to live as they pleased, isolated enough, yet, with a car, only ten minutes from Carmel. She was feeling stronger now. The rains had stopped. They drove to San Francisco, bought furniture, rugs, batiks. Soon everything was ready. Richard's many books, which had been stored, and other things she loved, arrived. It just came about that they moved into the new home on Nadia's birthday. They stayed together all day, sitting on the sun porch, taking in sea and soil and the light washed clean now, scintillating on every leaf, after the rains. Three humans together and the earth . . . beside the clangor of useless words, the whirring of uncentered minds, and all the confusion of an age prurient with ugliness, sloppy with meaningless activities, cancerous with monstrous selfishness. Beside all these things, yet within—ready to face it, accept it, absorb it if need be, that purification might be accomplished.

Three humans in the cottage.

Nadia begged to stay.

She felt miserable with her brother in their small crowded rooms. She sensed him going headlong into the claws of "the Ogre," as she said. The Hindu had left, but, however quickly Carmel usually forgot her many mind-lovers, that one had struck solid, greedy roots in the soil of a few dissatisfied beings. Peter had resisted long. He hated groups and talks; but his very self-centeredness was leading him insensibly into the thing one would think was the most remote from his nature. His apparent moral sturdiness was mostly fear, Nadia thought. He carried locked within his silences many Russian ghosts. Someday they would rush out. She could feel them peeping through the keyhole. No thanks, she was not eager to be near when they would parade out. Besides, did not Rania need her to keep the house? She was not able to attend to cleaning, cooking. It would wear her out. Boris had his work and Rania might just as well help him and leave all the material cares to her. Was it not the only sensible thing to do? She would not bother them, and as long as she would get room and board and some pieces of clothing, she would feel so happy.

Nadia begged to stay.

Three souls indrawn as one.

Against the world they stood. Peter had violently opposed his sister's going. He thought that after all that had been said it was disgraceful for Boris to condone such close intimacy. Perhaps he did not care! Perhaps he was happy to have his wife busy with a young girl! Boris became very pale. His answer was short, cutting. What kind of a foul mind must one have to throw such accusations at one's sister and friend? If that was his way, all right. There was room for all kinds in this world. But he might as well beware, lest he sink deeper into the astral mire with which he was surrounding himself. Nadia was of age. She was free. She had made her application the day before to become an American citizen, as he himself had done. Besides he was planning to adopt her legally, if it could be arranged. Peter sneered. That was the last stroke! A fine family they were making. Well, good luck to them! He would have nothing more to do with the whole business. But he was free to say what he thought. And he did. The Sarmananda group sucked him in still more powerfully. The cleavage accentuated itself. Something dark and heavy pressed upon the little town. It made individual egos feel more helpless, more chaotic, more frantically drawn toward any kind of wreckage to which they might hold on, desperately, like drowning men. It hung heavily, shattering every effort at unification, at communal cooperation. The little clans that constantly were forming withdrew more into stony isolation. Yet little wars raged, with bitterness on both sides, for this or that unimportant possession—newspapers, theaters, shops, societies.

Against it, three souls indrawn as one.

Not defeated, not withdrawing.

Boris opened the house to weekly receptions and discussions at which all willing ones were accepted, known or unknown, friend or foe. His car called on those unable to come otherwise; Nadia being active as a chauffeur as well as cook, help and maid. During the evenings he usually took some paragraphs from great spiritual books, ancient or modern, and developed the ideas recorded in the pregnant words. Few came at first. Mrs. Falkner, torn between her daughter and her own intuitive recognitions, was there, trying to cling to something stable on which she might perchance hang her shattered peace. Others appeared more or less regularly, drawn in by curiosity or genuine interest. Boris rented the theater and gave a series of three free public lectures on "What is Wholeness?" He did not mention any names. But it was clear to every one that his words were aiming powerfully at the doctrines spread by Sarmananda. First, he gave a philosophical interpretation of the last five thousand years, delineating the great periods subdividing this era, elucidating the meaning of each. He uncovered the significance of Krishna, Buddha, Jesus and more recent great Teachers; why they came, the keynote of their teachings, the perversions which befell these teachings. Then he discussed the fundamental bases of all great philosophies; the unity of all lives, the cyclic unfolding of the tide of being, the essential identity of all individualized selves with the universal Self. Lastly he analyzed methods of living, correcting misconceptions, stimulating his hearers into renewed effort at self-realization through fulfillment of congenital duties, through impersonal action. He showed the dangers facing all true spiritual search, the pitfalls confronting would-be occultists. He ended with a plea for common sense, for purity, for selflessness.

Not defeated, but a powerful affirmation.

A few rallied. With them, he and Rania worked in utter devotion.

—∞◇∞—

sacrifice of the seed

CHAPTER II

Weeks of steady, joyous work.

Boris was writing the first of a series of books which were to present a vast cycle of ideas covering the most significant aspects of human life and of the search for universal truths and fundamental values. He was writing methodically, summoning hour after hour words that would convey forcefully, directly, his lucid vision. Without waste, without undue effort, he was recording facts of the mind-world with which he was conversant, in which his being had been centered since early adolescence. He was recording. He did not claim to invent or imagine. He was a living pen stating coherently, vividly the inner destiny which he was as an Idea. The idea he was had grown through the destiny he had appeared to be; grown by opposition, by contrasts of shadow and light, grown into form, into human manifestation. The idea was eternal, cyclic, as an idea. The destiny was the progressively self-revealing image of the idea in the world of personalities. It was very simple, very explicit—for one who could lift his consciousness from the tumult of bodily chemicalizations, of racial and earthly affinities and repulsions. So few were able, alas!

While unfolding in his writings that idea which he was, he was telling his companions characteristic phases of the destiny through which he had come to formation. For long moments of quiet beauty they sat against the varnished trees washed clean for the celebration of spring, amidst the adolescent earth throwing out her love to space in multitudes of flowers. The resinous scent of the pines drew to itself the softer, indecisive fragrances of lupins and geraniums and of many wild gestures of the soil. It had power. It rose against the sea winds, salt-heavied and vibrant. And while slowly the green of the hills began to glow into sun browns and yellows, many weeks passed.

Of steady, concentrated, joyous work.

His tumultuous, rich destiny.

He was born in Moscow. His father, an aristocrat claiming descent from the Vikings who came with Rurik the Rodsman before the Tartar invasions—his mother, a woman from southern Russia whose ancestors had come from the old Parsee race. In him was brought to a focus the conflict of spiritual polarities. He was a true Moscovite. His youth had been brilliant and adventurous. He had lived many months on the Crimean estate of his mother. His body was weak and high strung at first. He had queer fevers which puzzled the doctors. He was passionately fond of children and Cossacks. They adored him. But with his relatives and aristocratic friends he was bitingly proud and commandeering. He went to school, but refused to work. He would fly into terrible rages and invented all sorts of things to upset the peace of the institution. His mother's death, soon after followed by his father's departure, came to him as a shock. First, he rebelled. Then a strange passionate mysticism took hold of him. Puberty had come. He fell ill. Physicians diagnosed some complicated internal disease. They operated upon him and to their amazement found nothing wrong. The two or three years that followed were years of intense yearning and distress. He wanted to die. He fell in desperate love with several girls. The girls did not really matter. But something was burning through him, and unable as he was to attune himself to the power of it, it was melting his very soul that rushed into every mold offered to it, like liquid iron. Then the hurts made him recoil in self-defense.

At that time he devoured books. Nietzsche became his god. He sneered at his previous mysticism. Away with all softness and love! He would be a master, master of himself, master of men. He invented subtle ways of proving to himself his mastery over his body and nerves. He inflicted injuries on himself in tense denial of pain. He walked long hours in absolutely dark forests, dominating his fears. He jumped into cold streams, when his body was shivering. Then he dreamt, long endless daydreams in which, rising from his actual position, he would inevitably in wondrous and varied ways conquer large portions of the earth, establish empires, build cities, and die, surrounded by thousands worshiping him, loving him . . . often on the top of some huge Asiatic or African mountain, whence he could feel the vast expanse of the earth which he had submitted and fecundated with power and magnificence.

Then he came to live with an aunt. She was a strong-willed, implacable and ambitious woman, who after having tried to rule her aristocratic circles and met sudden failure after some scandal, had withdrawn into occult studies. He was sent to her and she, sensing at once in him a power she could train for her own aims, had taken great interest in him and had entangled her life very closely with his. She captured his imagination. She was a woman to his taste, a powerful, determined creature. He followed her in her studies, in many more or less "occult" experiments. In Moscow and Petrograd a few secret circles and societies were to be found before the war. They joined one or two; they had strange dealings with people who came from Asia. Mysterious plots and plans were discussed. In the midst of all this the war came. It left him indifferent. He was passionately plunged in studies, in research. He left for Turkestan, partly to avoid the war consciousness, partly to get nearer to the center of Asia.

A series of strange adventures came to him. His aunt had been compromised in a big ammunition scandal. She fled to the Caucasus. He followed her. They both rode through the wild passes flying from men who wanted their death for State reasons. They experienced dreadful hardships; but it was an ecstatic adventure, this flight through snows, unknown valleys, then right into Armenia and Turkey. They were attacked by bandits. He dragged her, wounded, for miles, until he reached a small village. The woman died. As he was wondering whither to go, a Persian who was traveling with a small escort offered to take him along into Persia.

While going on slowly through mountainous and frozen countries, the Persian began to talk to him. Soon he found this man to be a renowned Bahai; once a Sufi teacher belonging to some secret order, he had thrown himself into the Bahai cause and was spreading a gospel of mystic devotion and eager love in the name of Abdul-Baha, with whom he had lived in Akka. An unforgettable trip this had been. Something in Boris had broken, something opened. The Persian was a living fire of love. It burned Boris's pride and harshness. All his tinsel power seemed to fall from him. He was left, naked, shivering in soul. He was twenty-five years old.

sacrifice of the seed

For a while he remained with the mystic in Persia. Months of metamorphosis, of rebirth. He suddenly craved humble tasks, service, complete self-abnegation. A passion for suffering, expiation, sacrifice seized him. He felt himself insignificant before his teacher and friend. "Ya Baha el Abba!" he would cry into the night, like the early Bahai martyrs. And the earth flew into him, and distended him; and he became humanity.

The Russian Revolution came. He burned to go. He wanted to fight with the people, to repair wrongs, to raise the great fervent banner of love amongst those who had suffered so desperately from hatred and insolence. His friend smiled, but let him go. He had to follow his destiny.

He found all his fortune and estates gone. When he arrived in the country where he had passed his youth, where he had owned large territories, he found an infuriated mob of peasants claiming revenge. He barely escaped death. A girl, whose life he had saved years before, protected him and fled with him. In Moscow he attempted to see revolutionists he had known. They were caught in the great fury, and the wheels of power smashed all past relations. Like steel girders tense with tremendous pressure, they were raw with work; they laughed at Boris's preachings; they shoveled him into strenuous, exasperating labor. He could not stand the barbaric strain of it. His nerves gave up. He asked to be sent to fight the Whites in Crimea, which he knew so well.

Months of hopeless war, desertion, atrocities on both sides. His soul sickened and he was ready to fall, a wreck. The girl, who had not left him, fell ill with typhoid fever. To help her die, he disobeyed orders, was left by the retreating Reds. Between the two armies death seemed certain. By sheer chance he succeeded in getting through the lines and fought his way to a steamer which lead him to Constantinople.

The months that followed were the darkest he experienced. He was parked with thousands of Russian refugees in wooden barracks exposed to the chilly winds that blew through the straits. The misery of these men and women who had known only luxury and grandeur was appalling. None could leave. They were welcome nowhere. Only women who married foreigners could leave. He saw a beautiful young girl who had been an attendant to the empress give herself in marriage to a French Negro just to escape the horror of these barracks. There was little food. There was disease. Men and women often lay bundled together trying to keep warm, trying to love, for a moment of forgetfulness! And they sang. And they danced; they died too, by the dozens.

He had accepted death. But instead came a man searching for him. He had a letter. It was from his Persian teacher. "Farewell, my son," read the letter. "I hope this will reach you. I am soon to enter the Kingdom of El-Abba. The breezes of peace are around me. I have not forgotten you. Now even, I see you among many sufferers. Come out of this death, my son. Rise into the light that is yours. The bird with bound wings cannot fly. May God the Mighty, the boundless, the compassionate, help you to soar into the heaven of dedication and to enter the Rizwan of certitude!"

Boris had asked in amazement how the messenger had found him. But no answer came. The mysterious man took him to a good hotel. While Boris was taking a bath, he heard the door of the room close. The man had left. On the table he found a large envelope with two thousand pounds and these words: "Do not look for me. Fulfill your destiny. This will help you find the way—if you are wise."

After a few days of rest Boris had decided to go to Egypt and then to India. Of his trip he told many wonderful experiences and how finally he had found in Ceylon his great teacher; a man who had

SACRIFICE Of THE SEED

attempted to regenerate Buddhism in the south, through a life of
utter purity, nobility and consecration. A great teacher. He had
traveled with him along the roads of India for five years, as a
Bikkhu, wearing the yellow robe, begging his food. What these
years had been could not be told. They had wandered toward the
northern regions, to Benares, to the Bo-tree from whose shadow
Gautama once had arisen to lead men, during forty years of perfect
teaching, "to the other shore." One day, the sage had looked into
Boris's eyes deeply for a long time in silence. And he had bid him
go to America and help the few who were ready to live, in the way
of nobility, the Aryan path of old, the eternal path that leads from
ignorance into certainty and peace.

A tumultuous, rich destiny.

—∞◇∞—

Now work was the fulfillment.

Rania and Nadia were swept into the steady rhythm of activity,
mental and physical. Ten, twenty letters came every day from the
many friends and disciples whom Boris had made in India, in Java
where he had tarried for a few months, and during his years of
constant traveling through the United States. Long answers were
expected; life problems demanded to be solved; little hearts were
resting in the hands of one who had faced life and had won. That
also was work, even the mere physical act of letter-writing. Most of
these letters Boris either dictated or sketched in their general
outlines to Rania who was typing them, slowly at first, but with
increasing speed and efficiency. Nadia also was learning typing and
shorthand during the few hours not taken by household cares, by
driving in and out, bringing in people who wanted to see Boris
and had no car. Besides there were a couple of hours reserved for
study, concentration. Both Rania and Nadia had to read and

179

meditate over certain works, making summaries, annotating, condensing for simpler exposition parts of more abstruse works. Nadia especially had yet little knowledge of philosophy or science. She had shunned the very thought of them when at school. But now they had become alive. She was caught in a powerful mental polarization. The rhythm of work flew into her openness that had become a vessel filled by great ideas growing into living realities.

Through work, fulfillment.

Rania had begun again to draw.

For many months it had seemed useless to her. But a new sense of form had developed in her. Her vehement imagination seemed to have condensed into a clear, Doric vision of being. Numbers and geometrical figures had begun to show their structural function to her essentialized perceptions. She studied everything she could find on Pythagorean ideas, Hambidge's works on Dynamic Symmetry, books on crystals, on plant growth, the laws of form and manifested being, the laws of cosmic development; these became to her fascinating studies. With a new and for the first time fully deliberate assurance—before, she had worked in a more "inspired," passive manner—she tried to produce forms which would be of eternal universal significance, archetypal forms of life. She perceived them in trees, rocks, flowers which she essentialized into their barest rhythms. She watched for them in human faces. She drew them in sharp yet supple outlines. She let herself construct poems of lines and masses and colors that told tragedies of cosmic parturitions. In these works all her passionate soul would flare with chiaroscural intensity; but passion become form and meaning, passion from which the personal vehemence had been purified—passion become cosmic energy, intensely coordinated organic power.

sacRiFice of the seed

Rania had begun again to draw.

From morning to evening, work.

Not a moment wasted, useless. But also relaxation in the sun, short drives in the hills, in the canyons, to escape the sea-fog gliding in with the summer, to release the body from mind-tensions; Nadia dancing in the wind, running wildly to the sea and plunging into the cold gray waters, with the strong power of waves stimulating the body resisting, leaping, using the dumb waters as a lever for rhythmic swaying. Relaxation, but positiveness. From one activity to another; a sense of mastery of functions, using them, but not being used by them; a clear understanding of bodily equilibrium, of mental laws. At the end, efficiency. Not the mechanical, soulless, destructive efficiency of modern experts; but the conquest of inertia and of molecular-emotional chemicalizations for the purpose of soul. The soul came into matter to learn, to order chaos into cosmos, and to lift up lesser lives. It meant purity of causation—with its corollaries, benevolence and compassion. It meant exactitude and thoroughness; it meant punctuality—so had Boris been taught by one whose life was a model of harmonious, benevolent activity. It was the eternal law, the one way of service. Being through doing, but doing illumined by being—made significant, pure, all-encompassing by the flame of soul bringing into every gesture and every deed, knowledge, love, universality.

Life had become a poem of work.

Months were its stanzas.

They passed in vivid procession with a richness that precluded monotony. To break the possible tenseness Boris decided to take a long trip to Yosemite and the Sierras. Nadia had never seen big mountains. It was a revelation. Rania remembered. She had lived beautiful weeks in contemplation of these huge masses with her old Johan. He was dying then; she, bursting with incoherent, sumptuous life. As she faced the same panoramas, she realized more deeply and accurately than she could have in any other way the change that had taken place in her. Johan—Boris. Happiness . . . but how different in substance; the old and the new! She had turned around herself. She had become her hidden self, the changeless face of the moon that looks toward Space, where there is no sun-glamor, where darkness and silence are divinity. She had become that silence and that darkness. Everything in her that had risen or glowed in exuberance had resolved itself into stonelike certitude, into dispassionate work. She had become a work, a destiny. As a destiny she could see, through all forms, into the destinies of these forms. Once the tremendous spectacles of the Sierras had roused in her fervid imagination, colossal visions of stone-dramas; her personality had made all things personal. Now she saw all things through the eyes of a destiny; she saw all things as forms, as equations of energy. Not dramas of personalities, but interplays of cosmic destinies.

Months, years—as stanzas of a destiny.

She was watching Nadia.

The girl's nature was so interestingly different from her own, yet so much the same. After the few moments of exhilaration caused by the eruption of such magnificences into her sensibility, Nadia had made all these terrific earth-visions her own. She had opened herself to them and absorbed them as a matter of fact. Rania had been drunk with them for weeks, when they had burst upon her years ago. They had aroused a glorious personal reaction. Nadia had been stirred nervously at first, then she had accepted the natural intensity as a fact. She did not oppose anything to it, not even that which would be necessary to create joy. She had found it there. The moment a little nervous flurry had subsided, it was all settled. She had added that much of the universal being to herself. She had recognized it. She felt richer from it; and it too was richer from having been recognized. That also was destiny; a meeting of self-equating energies. And Nadia was essentially that, an openness of self-equating energies, a wholeness always in the making, living in impersonal naturalness, with strong nervous reactions almost instantly vanishing because underneath them there was nothing to oppose anything. Only life to recognize and grow into life.

Rania was watching her.

Nadia loved Boris.

But such a love was also of a clear, unopposing, cosmic nature. It reminded her of what she had read of love in ancient Aryan books, love as of the elements, love as a face of fulfillment: "He is Vishnu, she is Shri. She is language, he is thought. He is reason, she is sense. She is duty, he is right. He is patience, she is peace. He is chant, and she is note. She is fuel, he is fire. She is glory, he is sun. She is orbs, he is space. . . " There was nothing to say of such a love, nothing to act out. It was a necessity of being. Rania had come to Boris as a soul-cry that was nearly submerged. She had found in him the link she had lost, that which had cemented her into wholeness. He had shown her the path that is unique, explained to her its uniqueness, upheld her into its strenuous treading. They were companions both, hands within hands; he only farther on. But Nadia and Boris were one in a more cosmic sense. He had adopted her. She was note, he was chant. She was orbs, he was space. They were a uniqueness of destiny.

They all knew it.

Three humans equated into destiny.

—∞◇∞—

The translucent fall came.

It brought perfection to a relation which was total and simple. There was no fog in it, no necessity for words, those masks of reality. Sky, waters, earth united in human significance: star-container and fecundator–the ever-moving, ever-absorbing, ever-cleansing sea–the fruit-bearing earth, a fragment of sky made tangible, made meaningful by limitations and mass. The work of the three had grown to a point of climactic intensity. Boris's first book was nearly finished and he was outlining a broad plan of activities to spread in many countries the basic ideas which he felt constituted the keynotes of the emerging new and global human society. Rania was absorbed by the ever-increasing correspondence connected with the furtherance of this plan. Her creative work filled the balance of the strenuous days. She was working on a series of panels which were to be incorporated some day in a sort of university-temple of which Boris had dreamt and which might become a living center of civilization. She had envisioned for them a new medium, a combination of black-and-white and bas-relief techniques. Transparent surfaces lighted from within were to be incorporated in the panels. It was the ultimate development of Western chiaroscuro revivified by a deeper sense of cosmic harmony.

The translucent fall came.

The seed had matured.

Human nature in harmony with earth-nature; yet not *of* this earth–hardly even *in* the earth!–but *through* the earth. Human nature focused as a channel of materialization, as a vehicle of activity. Equilibrium had been reached, a threefoil. Its stem reached to the source of life. It had grown against the darkness, against the decaying emotionality of those who had been instruments of fate to bring about the conjunction; who had been thrown out of the sacred circle by the centrifugal fever of their own cravings and fears. As the seed reached maturity, the leaves which had conditioned its substance were withering. A strange dissatisfaction and morbidity seemed to have pervaded the sensitive existences gathered in Carmel. Two young people had committed suicide. Accidents had occurred. No effort to bring about communal enterprises escaped prompt disintegration. Some individuals had taken refuge in sophistication or sarcastic irony; others had withdrawn into the shade of book reading, in the monotonous routine of an easy but drab existence, bitter at heart in spite of a careless indifference and "Why bother about humanity?" Others were rushing more hectically than ever from this to that novel excitement in politics, religion, or art. The Sarmananda group had grown and deepened its deleterious work.

The seed had matured.

Winter was coming.

There must come a winter for every seed. There must come that which protects and shields the seed toward spring, that which indeed gives its life and absorbs the hatred of winter for life, that mysterious essence which is the sacrificial aspect of life. It made the seed possible. It keeps the seed growing in the hidden ways of winter. It takes upon its heart the pangs of Christ-birth, the furor of all the Herods who represent that part of the race which bitterly had died, which had become death incarnate. Rania understood. Boris did not speak of such things. They must not be spoken within the seed. But every particle of it must know from within, in the silence. There can be no false sentimentality, no frightened clinging to a static happiness.

Winter was coming.

Centrifugal tensions were crucifying the seed.

A strange nervousness and weariness took hold of Nadia. The walls of the cottage were like huge batteries she did not dare touch, so heavy they felt with electricity. Something beat upon her. She would run out and dash off along the coast, or speed dangerously in the car. The pressure of constant concentration began to show itself. Even Boris became irritable, when people gathering to hear him asked questions. The future was stabbing the present at the heart. It was breaking the One into divergent paths. No rain came. The land was dry, dust overwhelming. A cold, chilly wind blew continuously, that made Rania ache unceasingly. Sciatica, neuritis, insomnia: she fought them desperately, always absorbed in work, typing letters until her arms refused to move, sitting, her face contracted by pain, her nerves knotted and inhibiting the bodily functions. It was a tense year. Unknown diseases, accidents, scandals were crowding in the news of every day. The end of a cycle, Boris explained. The worst might have yet to come.

Tensions breaking asunder the seed.

Nadia looked at her elders with tears.

Things were coming to a head. She felt it. Her love for Rania seemed almost unable to bear it. What? She could not tell. But the wheel was turning, bleeding to death time, whose moments were flowing spasmodically, blood from a deep wound. Oh, the pity of our great loves, when destiny severs the joined units—yet there is no hatred, no indifference, nothing to give an emotional reason to the tragedy, the inescapable fulfillment that is death. Nadia could not bear it. Yet she knew all rebellion to be useless. Something had to happen. A deep fatality was forcing everyone to make some final, awesome because sacred, choice. It involved the whole Carmel group. It might involve some much greater consummation. Somehow it centered around Rania. She was the one who had brought Boris and Nadia together. Thanks to her, financially, they had been able to work all together in comfort and wonderful isolation, yet nearness. In many deeper ways she seemed the pivotal reality, as the sea is the pivotal substance of planetary destiny. Out of it, organized life grows into manhood. It receives the death of continents. It is the balancing rhythm of climates, of winds and telluric destinies.

Nadia looked at her elders with tears.

Toward Christmas the pressure increased.

Hilda had been the center of the Sarmananda group; and she was falling deeper still into the quicksands of her own repressions. The group met secretly at night and tried to carry on the work of "becoming wholeness" by interchange of magnetism, group concentration during long minutes of rapt silence, and calling upon some "center of wholeness" to take possession of the vessel thus built out of their complementary and supposedly harmonized lives. The results were soon quite appalling. They were such as follow mediumship of a certain type, plus all the devouring tensions of sex repression. Sarmananda had taught them to transmute their sex force by such equilibration of magnetisms. What could it do but bring about acute conditions of neurosis and psychic hysteria? Hilda and Robert especially, playing as they did with physical attraction exacerbated by constant proximity and wilful concentration on "transmutation"—in their case merely hyper-excitation with no release—had reached a point of near hysteria.

Toward Christmas the pressure increased.

It broke suddenly.

One day Hilda met Nadia on the street. Hilda was with Robert and a couple of girls from out of town. One asked who Nadia was. What Hilda said was so vile, it was such a base calumny about the life of Boris and Rania as well, that Nadia stopped abruptly and in sullen tones asked her to repeat her words. She did, with added sarcasm. Nadia lost her head and struck Hilda so violently that she fell to the street and injured her arm slightly. The incident stirred the whole little town. Nadia rode home in mad despair. She was not going to stay. She could not bear it. There must be an end to it or to her. She would go anywhere, do any job. It was too much.

The pressure had broken.

Rania and Boris had a long talk alone.

The work had to go on in some other way. The incident meant nothing new in itself, but it was a hand pointing out to some necessary decision. Boris had not expected to go away on tour so soon. He was still waiting for some final answer from a group in New York concerning the organization of a center of teaching which would be the first milestone in a general movement for the unification of Eastern and Western thought. That would mean his traveling a great deal, lecturing, meeting people and rousing interest in big cities, European as well as American. Perhaps the time was ready. Should they leave all three for the east?

But Rania refused to go.

sacrifice of the seed

She would stay in Carmel.

Someone had to remain there. Not only to receive and forward mail and attend to many practical details which would be necessary, but above all not to desert the place. She was not one to leave the battlefield as one vanquished. Boris and Nadia would go. Their task was clear. They were one great effort, one great will to serve, one channel. Boris could not go alone. He needed a secretary, a companion, to relieve him of physical and material preoccupation. She had enough money left to finance their trip. She would rent the cottage and take a cabin somewhere near, the upkeep of which would be light. It did not matter how simple it would be. Besides, she was not strong enough to travel. She would make them waste time and energy. And there would not be enough money for the three of them just now. Later perhaps, when things would be settled in the east, she would join them. But at present she saw her duty clear

She would stay in Carmel.

Thus the sacrifice was consummated.

After a month of preparation and forced work, Boris and Nadia left Carmel for the east. They would carry on the message and mission that were theirs. Rania would take care of the work in Carmel as well as she could, upholding the ideal at the center of an ever-spreading darkness. Yes, she would hold on, tightly, grimly. She was not afraid. They need not be sad for her. She knew how to stand alone at her post of destiny. To them, the great adventure of conquest and fecundation. She, too, had her work. Boris had given her direction and meaning. Through him, she had become poised in destiny, a destiny beyond form, name and utterance. Now she would make to him the gift of self and the gift of love, and thus she would be free, equated. She was giving Nadia to him. Were they not one? Oh, yes, of course she would love to be with him always, travel with him, help him. But was not her broken body the very negation of such a dream? So, why waste sentiment against a destiny for which she was responsible? She had known passion and human love. She had known the earth and its glorious selfhood. Now it was time to forget the earth and become stone—to be the cornerstone deep within the ground upholding in darkness the towering structure. Thus she would pay her debt to life, the debt of passion-torn youth. That she might live, one man had died. Hers now was the gift. Thus harmony would be re-established and she would be "free."

The sacrifice would be consummated to the full.

Go ye, builder and apprentice!

She bid them both success and happiness, with her strong lips and her strong hands. She saw them off in the morning. The crusaders left to reconquer the holy truth that men have crucified and forsaken for countless centuries. They looked at her who stood in stoic firmness, as the train sped on. Nadia fell sobbing into Boris's arms. The roads had opened for them. Great, arduous roads of struggling fervor, of staunch bravery. The roads had closed upon Rania. Alone, she remained, oh, drearily alone, facing hatred or indifference, facing illness that she felt had been but pushed aside by the intensity of harmonious work, facing poverty, and perhaps death. The cottage was rented. She had to move back to Carmel, near the Point; where darkness was greatest, where the black pillar she used to see and had almost forgotten, was staying. At the center of it. How could one wipe out the dark, but by absorbing it in one's own body with smiling heroic soul?

Go ye, builder and apprentice!

SACRIFICE OF THE SEED

The madonna remains, love that is strong, unfaltering; the stone, upon which darkness prevails not; the sea that washes clean the stench of human waste.

—∞◇∞—

CHAPTER III

The drought continued.

For nearly a year practically no rain had fallen. The soil was hard and barren, the hills seemed to moan brown sighs under the cutting winds. Nights were unnaturally clear. The sky had a harsh incandescent quality. Fever seemed to ooze from the tense earth. Cattle were dying, and epidemics were spreading among the people, diseases which were said to be of Oriental origin. They struck one suddenly with stabbing pains in the joints, pains so excruciating that one would often fall unconscious in the midst of ordinary gestures.

The drought continued.

It wore out resistance.

An uncanny sense of suffocation was in the air. One breathed more heavily. The water was rare and tasted raw and brittle, unliquid. The fluid virtue had gone out of it. Dust settled everywhere. Only the sea rose as ever toward the sand. It brought moisture, bitter moisture, to the earth. It had its peace and its fury. It could smile indifferently to the sun. But men have gone far from the sea. They have craved the sun. The sun fever hollowed the strongest.

It wore out resistance.

Sun blindness is darkness.

It means fever and exhaustion. It racks one. It corrodes the forms of life, greedy for all fluidic essence. Rania felt like an old Salton Sea dried out into the deserts—barren sands molded with grey-white salt moss. Some strange process of disintegration hidden for months was suddenly revealed in a hollowness which stirred pain everywhere in her body, sucked dry all organs and corroded the nerves.

Sun blindness is darkness.

She refused to give up.

She carried on accumulating work, answered letters, typed manuscripts which had to be ready for the printer. She sat at her worktable insistently with tense will, forgetting pain. Her face became drawn out. She could hardly do her housework. A few friends helped her at times. But few they were who stood faithful, now that Boris had ceased to be a magnet to draw them, now that the wildest tales were spread openly by Hilda, infuriated by the scene with Nadia, in which Rania was shown as a pervert, a seductress of young girls.

She refused to give up.

She was to be a standard.

The standard would be held upright as long as there was power in her will, as long as the nerves would stay tight. She had offered all she had, all she was to the work that was being pushed by two humans she loved and trusted beyond death. When they had left, she had known it would be the last time she would see them, as bodies. But she was with them, every moment. She lived in this oneness of destiny. There was nothing left in her to rebel or to bewail.

She had become a standard.

Her life divided itself once more into two parts.

At night—dreams or superphysical reality, who knew?—she would be with Boris and Nadia as fully as before. They would talk, study together, perform some mysterious actions the symbolism of which often seemed clear, often seemed veiled and confused. Then, the day saw her work as an instrument at her table, ceaselessly typing, sending to distressed ones strength, urging them to keep on, to see it through, to become seeds also, standards, destinies. Even then, her inner life was real, much beyond mechanical gestures, beyond brain-coalesced words. The thoughts arose, vivid, unavoidable, relentless. The hands obeyed. That bodily life was merely a process of work. It had become almost automatic; while the reality of living had its seat entirely beyond.

Her life divided itself once more.

Was there even pain?

A sense of tense energy seemed to dull sufferings that would have been otherwise unbearable. They had become so constant that they had reached a rhythm of their own of which she was hardly conscious, like that of breathing. She had become a machine to suffer, much as the lungs are machines to breathe. Yet the thoughts went on; ever new realizations, deeper meanings were won and expressed, and assimilated into soul—even though nerves suffered, bodily chemicalizations were like explosives restrained within the body frame only by a terrific hardening of the will, and the rhythm of racial or individual destiny proceeded unimpeded.

A coercion of pain.

—∞◇∞—

Suddenly the rains.

They flowed like cataracts. The passion of rain shook pines and bushes, rocks and humans. Streets turned into gorges thunderous with liquid possessions, furrowing the sand, eructating mud into the vehement sea. The dampness penetrated everything. Wood was so wet it refused to burn. As there was no gas in Carmel, heating became difficult, save for suffocating oil stoves which Rania could not endure. It was too much. She had to lie in bed wrapped in electric pads, shivering, teeth chattering.

The rains, the demented rains.

And disease spread.

It came slowly testing one man here, a child there, snapping a clerk at his desk, piercing with shrieking pains a barber sharpening his razor. It seemed contagious; yet no one could know how it was spread and what to do. The bones were attacked. Few died, but a terrific weakness was left in those who recovered; they were hardly able to stand straight. One of the first to go was Mrs. Falkner. She had been for months in a dreary state of depression, broken by

Hilda's conduct. Rania summoned strength to visit her. People were afraid. Even Hilda ran away. But Rania stood, and helped her to die.

Disease spread.

It had not crossed the mountains yet.

Rania had long, strong letters from her companions. They exhorted her. They poured their love into words that made her weep with communion. Oh, was she not with them completely, irrevocably–a great fire flaming forth to that which they also were? A fire that might bring regeneration to a world suffocated by craving and selfishness. Their love! How she knew herself in it! It rose, luminous, with radiant purity; a consecration, a strong diamond cutting all softness, all impurities away, focusing light rays into star clusters. They would carry on. They would rise on her death. They would withstand fatigue and disease.

It was never to cross the mountains.

She was tortured but fell not.

Weeks of utter solitude and darkness wrenched her, body and soul. She stared for endless hours at the low roof. She saw through it visions. She had almost left the earth. Her body, used to pain, resisted the disease better than many strong physiques. The epidemic was short. She had helped many around her. But she had to lie down. Even in her bed, she found strength to write, to send words of cheer to sufferers.

She was tortured, but fell not.

—∞◇∞—

SACRIFICE OF THE SEED

Then Sarmananda came back.

People were recovering from the shock of death. Strange nervous languor haunted many. An emptiness, physical and psychic. They were like shadows, weakly moving—because their brains had no sustenance beyond the chemicals of the earth, and the earth was still sick, even though May had come with belated florescence, with a fervid haste to blossom, to sing life in denial of death.

Sarmananda came back.

His fame had grown.

Boris wrote he was constantly meeting groups of enthusiasts trying to practice his perverted teachings, thinking to find wholeness in sex mysticism and the damming of unnaturally aroused passions. The true ideas were thrown topsy-turvy, unfocused, misapplied The body was worshiped. The body became God. People rushed for supernal experiences, which lead but to psychic monstrosity and to the reversion and perversion of natural impulses into mental demonisms. The group ideal was distorted. Group selfishness and group lust were taking the place of individual selfishness and lust. A subtler form of mediumship opened minds and hearts to sinister ingresses. The astral world was rushing through the bethinned partition of normal consciousness into the subconscious. Yet the blind crowded to hear Sarmananda.

His fame was wide.

Once more he took Carmel by force.

He welded his weakened group into an instrument of power, dynamizing them by his relentless personality. He became as a renovator after the hectic weeks of disease. Forcefully he banked

197

on the craving of people for health. Health was his servant. No one who lived whole could be ill. He thundered against physicians, preachers: they drugged people, accentuating the negation instead of building up complementary energies and restoring equilibrium. It sounded true, convincing. Indeed his mind was a keen blade; he understood the laws of life—but his monstrous ego-will forever sought to wrench from their destinies all his followers, to increase his own power and fill his insatiable spiritual void.

He took Carmel by force.

Still a few rebelled.

Saner minds had seen the deleterious effects of his method upon the group of his followers. Hilda's conduct had been shameful during the epidemic. She had let her mother die without a word, without any attention. Rania's strength and devotion had roused admiration. A slow, yet definite reaction was setting in. A few older friends who had listened to Boris gathered around her sickbed. Something ought to be done to awaken the minds of people as to what really was being done in the secret reunions of the Sarmananda group. Boris should be there to confront the Hindu and expose him.

A few rebelled.

Rania was very ill.

But she saw her duty. Was she not of the race of warriors? Must not the warrior fight to his last drop of blood? It was not enough to carry a standard and not be shaken. There came times when action, quick and strong, was necessary. Boris was away, fighting the battle where his destiny had led him. But *she* was in Carmel. She heard the call. She would rise. She would fight, as her mother had fought the wolves to save her. She would fight unto death . . . to save the few child-souls strong enough to cling to the tree of salvation which she would have grown for them out of the roots of her own being now fulfilled in crucifixion, as once she had thought it fulfilled in human passion.

Rania was very ill.

But Soul knows no illness.

She flung an open challenge to Sarmananda. There should be a series of debates between him and her on all the main tenets of his doctrines. She threw at him precise, definite accusations—charges of demoralization, of fallacious interpretation of true teachings. Newspapers printed them. A huge scandal smells good to the press. Sarmananda hesitated. His pupils wanted him to show Rania up. Why, she could not stand the confrontation with his powerful mind! It would be the end of this silly Khsantianoff family affair which had been such nonsense in Carmel. Sarmananda feared arguments. Like most autocrats he was really afraid of any real show of power. He was clairvoyant enough to sense Rania's soul strength. He accepted the challenge in a sarcastic answer. All the while he was bending all his occult knowledge and using his group in order to attack in psychic-astral ways the woman who dared brave him.

But Soul has power.

Rania resisted, strong in faith and purity.

She was burned night and day by mysterious fires she could sense darting toward her like red-iron arrows, sizzling into her flesh of soul. The torment of it was unbelievable. For hours she remained in meditation, linking herself spiritually, almost tangibly, with

Boris and with the Great Ones who stand behind any clear fight
for truth and love. She forged between herself and them a chain of
light along which strength and power flowed that toned up her
breaking body. With an intensity of mental concentration which
verged on ecstasy, she held the thought and the image of the light
whose rays they are, as a burning glow. She knew that they
watched. Was she not but a consecrated servant, a common soldier
in their army?

She was strong with the power they are.

And the battle began on the plane of men.

Face to face they stood. A huge massive man in yellow tunic—a
drawn-out, emaciated woman leaning on crutches. She began to
speak. First in tired, low tones. But as he started to answer,
something happened that upstrained her in heroic transfiguration.
Some Presence had come that had flowed through her. She was it;
yet not altogether it. She heard words her lips sounded forth with
a power that made her body tremble, like a pipe under the onrush
of high-pressured steam. She thought of Boris. Yet, it came from
beyond Boris. Oh, it was the three of them as unity, the three
dynamized by the fourth, the one Power of which, as a threefold
seed, they were the earthly vehicle. The realization of it, of the
significance of it, the glory and destiny of it, burned her,
enraptured her.

The battle was raging on the plane of men.

Rania won.

Sarmananda gave inadequate answers. Visibly he got himself
entangled in arguments which had no meaning. To the precise,
direct questions of Rania he answered evasively, then sarcastically,

then violently. At last he flew into a rage. The huge frame tore up and down the stage foaming hatred at the pale woman who seemed transfigured into some ecstatic countenance. It became so ugly, so painful, that a few people in the compact audience left, openly protesting. The chairman of the debate, an impartial scientist of renown who lived near Carmel, brought the meeting to a close, with ironic words aimed at the Hindu's behavior.

Rania won.

—∞◇∞—

And now a prostrated body lies on a couch in the little camp cabin while the heavy fog rolls in from the sea.

Rania, the woman, is broken and dying. The standard has been kept, the destiny well-fulfilled. What matters a body which no longer can breathe?

The body coughs and sweats in awesome agony. The life tide is receding. Soon it will have left entirely a frame of earth substances shattered by too much light.

It is life that kills from being too rich, from flowing so strongly into destiny that limits are melted into boundlessness.

But the darkness that falls is heavy with tortures. The powers of hate can do their task well, now that the soul is alone, her mission fulfilled.

They tear through the dark of the world beyond. Like ferocious wolves they rush on and foam to rend the exhausted soul that was named Rania.

"The wolves! The wolves! . . . " She shrieks, the dying one. Strong and fierce she stands against a tree to lash the beasts that growl death at her face.

They grab her legs. They leap at her throat. The heroic hands that had worked well collapse. A heart that was love faints and all is dark.

Still, the tree has grown out of roots of will. The tree strains its huge branches to stars that yet glimmer through the fog.

The tree is strong, strong, as strong as was Rania—strong to bear children that will be saved at dawn when light rises.

"Be strong! Be strong, my children! Be strong!" The words have rung out of dying lips. The words have power.

"Oh, be strong! be strong! . . . my children."

—∞◇∞—

This edition of 5000 copies was printed by Stecher-Traung
& Schmidt of San Francisco on Glatfelter paper. Text set
in Garamond by Dharma Press on a Harris-Intertype. Running heads handset in Libra by the Mackenzie & Harris
foundry. Remaining display type handset in Garamond by
the Unity group. Fifty copies of this edition have
been selected, numbered and signed
by the author.

A PARTIAL LIST OF BOOKS BY THE AUTHOR

✷

ASTROLOGICAL THEMES FOR MEDITATION. C.S.A. 1973

AN ASTROLOGICAL MANDALA. Random House 1973

MY STAND ON ASTROLOGY. Seed Center, Palo Alto, 1972

THE PLANETARIZATION OF CONSCIOUSNESS: From the Individual to the Whole. Servire 1970; Harper & Row 1972

BIRTH PATTERNS FOR A NEW HUMANITY. Servire 1969; in a new edition as ASTROLOGICAL TIMING: The Transition to a New Age. Harper & Row 1972

THE PRACTICE OF ASTROLOGY. Servire 1967; Penguin 1970

THE LUNATION CYCLE: A Key to the Understanding of Personality. Servire 1967; Shambala Publications 1971

THE PULSE OF LIFE: New Dynamics in Astrology. MacKay 1943; Shambala Publications 1970

THE ASTROLOGY OF PERSONALITY: A Reformulation of Astrological Concepts and Ideals in terms of Contemporary Psychology & Philosophy. Lucis Press 1936; Doubleday 1970